A VERY BLACKWELL CHRISTMAS

CHRISTINA ROSS

A Very Blackwell Christmas is a new book set in the *Annihilate Me* universe. It's an extension of the series with more than 3.5 million books sold worldwide in six different languages.

Below is the reading order of the *Annihilate Me* series as well as the titles of my three stand-alone novels.

ANNIHILATE ME, VOL. 1
ANNIHILATE ME, VOL. 2
ANNIHILATE ME, VOL. 3
ANNIHILATE ME, VOL. 4
ANNIHILATE ME, HOLIDAY EDITION

UNLEASH ME, VOL. 1
UNLEASH ME, VOL. 2
UNLEASH ME, VOL. 3

ANNIHILATE HIM, VOL. 1
ANNIHILATE HIM, VOL. 2
ANNIHILATE HIM, VOL. 3

IGNITE ME

ANNIHILATE HIM, HOLIDAY

A DANGEROUS WIDOW

ANNIHILATE THEM
ANNIHILATE THEM: HOLIDAY

ACKNOWLEDGMENTS

For my friends, my father, and my mother.
And especially for my readers, who mean the world
to me.
Thank you for following the *Annihilate Me* series into its
next chapter.

ONE
BARBARA

December
New York City

I was seated behind my desk on the fifty-first floor of the Wenn Enterprises building—crunching down on a cube of ice while minding my own damned business—when I heard them coming my way.

I knew it was Jennifer and Lisa, because when it came to those two? When they were on a mission, as they clearly were now? They sounded like a couple of brood mares strapped into two pairs of Manolo Blahniks as they steamrolled down the hallway toward me.

And what fresh hell are they about to darken my doorway with today? I mused as I looked across my spacious office at the open door. *What could possibly be the matter now? Oh right! We're on the cusp of Christmas. So naturally this must be about that.*

How utterly predictable.

And then there they were—flushed! At least Jennifer looked presentable in the black Prada leather pencil skirt she'd paired with a long-sleeve cashmere sweater. But Lisa? My perfect size zero? She looked only passable in a pair of dark skinny jeans and a white blouse. Yes, she was a writer who spent most of her days huddled in what I imagined was some dark, lifeless room where she banged out her ridiculous zombie novels, so I decided to give her outfit a pass, if only because her hair and makeup were on point.

At least she'd tended to them before she'd dared to come see me.

"What's the issue?" I asked before either of them could speak. "I have a meeting in ten minutes, so make it quick."

"Ten minutes?" Lisa said in frustration. "This is going to take at least an hour to sort out."

I looked at Jennifer for confirmation.

"An hour?" I asked.

"At least an hour," Jennifer said with a sigh. "None of this is good."

"For whom?"

"Potentially for all of us."

With a raised eyebrow, I leaned toward my desk, placed my right elbow on top of it, and rested my chin in the palm of my hand as I gazed at each of them. "*All* of us?" I said. "Pray tell, how did *I* ever get swept up into whatever nightmare you two have devised, and why is it going to take at least an hour to sort out?"

"It's Ethel," Lisa said. "Tank's mother."

"Thank you for the reminder, my dear," I said. "I mean, as if there's another *Ethel* in my life."

"Anyway, she and Harold have decided to come here of all places for Christmas. To Manhattan—where they've never been. And while they're here, they have no plans to get a hotel room. Instead, they want to shack up with Tank and me at *our home*! Ethel called this morning to break the 'good news' to me. Jesus, Barbara, you know what went down between that woman and me at my wedding. You know how she was with me. Sure, things seemed to have settled down since then, but who the hell knows what that holy roller is going to bring our way over Christmas? Before they even arrive, I'm officially on record for calling all of this an unmitigated disaster."

"And I'm telling each of you this isn't something I can handle right now," I said firmly. "There is, after all, work to be done. So how about this? Are you two available for dinner tonight?"

"I am," Jennifer said.

"I totally am—Tank will understand," Lisa said.

"Then how about if we dine at Le Bernadin and figure this out before both of you have the gall to develop frown lines in front of me?"

"Le Bernadin?" Jennifer said. "We'll never get in."

"I'm Blackwell," I said. "And *you* are Jennifer Wenn, the wife of a billionaire. Of course we'll get in, so plan to meet me here at seven sharp. I'll ask Cutter to drive us. I understand we'll be dining unfashionably early, and even though I detest the thought of that, tomorrow is a busy day, so it is what it is."

I stood up from my desk and shot Lisa a look. "And

for the love of God, Lisa, please find something suitable to wear. Because *je refuse* to show up at *that* restaurant with anyone who looks like you do now."

"I'm in crisis!" she bellowed.

"To be decided," I said. And then I stopped short and looked coolly at her. "But I will say your outfit is."

AS EXCLUSIVE AS Le Bernadin was, naturally we got a table—and one of the best, if only because when my assistant called to make a reservation, the staff likely mooned over the idea that Jennifer Wenn—wife of Alexander Wenn—would rather like to dine there tonight.

This was the city's original temple of haute French seafood—and it had maintained its gilded reputation for decades.

With white tablecloths, decorous service, and a jackets-required policy in the main dining room, the space remained formal but with a slightly modern twist thanks to its sleek leather banquettes and a twenty-four-foot mural of a tempestuous sea by Brooklyn artist Ran Ortner.

When we arrived, we checked our coats and then were greeted by the handsome host, who led us to one of the banquettes beneath the mural. It was the perfect spot to dine because it was *the* place in the restaurant to see—and to be seen.

Because Jennifer was famous in this city, even this storied crowd couldn't help but turn to look at her as we took our seats and asked the host to bring us three martinis. Since I knew I was about to get into the mud with these two, I sweetly asked for my martini to be made dirty.

When the drinks arrived, I was happy to see that it was.

"Here's to us," Jennifer said as she lifted her glass toward the center of the round table.

"Don't you mean here's to the unnecessary steaming pile of drama Lisa is about to unload at this table?" I asked as I touched glasses with them before taking a sip of the ice-cold cocktail. It was beyond perfect. In fact, it was divoon.

"There's nothing unnecessary about it," Lisa said with a toss of her pretty blonde hair. Thankfully, she'd upped her game and had changed into the lovely black Dior suit I'd suggested she purchase in the fall. "Even I couldn't have written a plot twist as evil as Ethel darkening my doorstep on Christmas—and for an entire week, no less. I can see it now. She's probably going to ply me with more audiobooks about all the ways I'm going to burn in hell because I write about the undead. Please tell me how I can get out of this. I seriously need some help here."

"Where does Tank stand when it comes to this?" I asked.

"He's as uneasy about it as I am," she said. "I understand it's been two and a half years since we got married at their farm in Prairie Home, NObraska, but let's not kid ourselves—the wounds still sting on both sides."

"You haven't seen them since, have you?" I asked.

"I haven't, but Tank has."

"Oh dear."

"I know, but I was on deadline and couldn't go with him."

"I can only imagine how that was received."

"Tank said everything went well. I say the reason everything went well was because I chose not to go. But whatever. Now Ethel either wants to try to wash it all away with a visit over the holidays or to stir up even more shit. I think it could be the latter. I don't trust her."

"You have no reason to trust *that* one," Jennifer said.

"Well, I do agree with that," I said. "Ethel is a wolf. But I will caution you on this, Lisa—if you shut her out, plan on her taking it personally, which won't bode well for your tenuous relationship with her. I know you think a lot of her husband—"

"I love Harold."

"Then you also must consider how this will affect your relationship with him. And how all of this will impact Tank, which of course it will. His mother will not only resent you if her little whim to spend Christmas with you isn't fulfilled but also it will affect him. Is that something you want to live with?"

"What are you saying?" she asked me.

"I think if you want to keep the peace in the family, both of you are going to have to suck it up and welcome Ethel and Harold into your home. What choice do you have? None. But you already knew that, didn't you?"

She took a long pull from her martini and then shrugged. "She just sprang this on me today. There was a part of me that was hoping that somehow the three of us could get together tonight and scheme my way out of it." She sighed. "But you're right. She's got me cornered, because if I don't go along with this, it will be just another scar on our relationship."

"So you'll do it?" I asked.

"For every reason you pointed out, I guess I have no choice. But what about Christmas Eve? Jennifer and Alex have always hosted. Hell, it's become a tradition where all of us either gather at their home in Maine or at their apartment here. This year Tank and I were going to offer to host. But with Ethel meddling in my home, it's just not going to be the same because she'll feel she has some sort of power over me there, if only because I'm married to her son."

"Look," Jennifer said. "It's fine. Alex and I would love to host again. That way, Ethel will have to be on her best behavior because she'll be on *my* turf."

"I appreciate that, Jennifer, but you've done it so often, it's not fair for you to take on that responsibility again."

"I couldn't agree more," I said. "And need I remind both of you that it was only three years ago that I had one martini too many and pitched headfirst into Jennifer's tree, sending ornaments crashing to the floor? No? I didn't think so because I was a goddamned horror show. As I tried to compose myself, I remember thinking, 'You're not slurring, darling—you're merely speaking in cursive. No one will notice the difference.' But they did. We spent the last two Christmases in Maine. But if we have Christmas Eve at Jennifer and Alex's apartment again, everyone will be reminded of what became of *me* that year—distraught over a goddamned man."

"Marcus," they said at once.

"Yes, Marcus," I said. "I made a fool of myself after I broke things off with him—and everyone witnessed it. *Je refuse* to evoke that memory in anyone this year. *Je refuse!*"

"Then Tank and I will do it," Lisa said. "We'll put our heads together, try our best, and get it done. Ethel likes to cook. Maybe I can keep her busy with the food."

"Come again?" I said to her.

"I'll distract Ethel and keep her out of my hair by chaining her to the kitchen."

"Are you suggesting you won't have this event catered?"

"Well, I mean I could, if that's what everyone would prefer," she said.

"Here's why that matters to me," I said. "That woman knows I intentionally poisoned her with lilacs at your wedding. We set her up, Lisa. We knew she was severely allergic to them. We buried them deep within a bouquet of other flowers so that she wouldn't see them—and she didn't. But after she took one whiff of our little flower bomb, the woman broke out into hives and nearly didn't make it to her own son's wedding. You think she's forgotten that? That she still doesn't hold a grudge to this day because of that stunt? You're a fool if you do—and you're also a fool if you think she won't poison the lot of us if she's in charge of making the food. I can see the little Bible-thumper now, sprinkling rat poison onto everything. She's not above it!"

"Seriously?" Jennifer said as she sipped her martini. "Rat poison, Barbara? Really?"

"Or worse, because time doesn't heal all wounds, my dear. That woman hates some of us that much."

"I don't think she hates Alex or me," she said.

"That's because people *like* you."

"Something you might aspire to one day."

"Never. *J'adore* being feared."

"I'm not having Jennifer and Alex host again this year, Barbara," Lisa said. "I mean, come on. There will be too many people there—Jennifer and Alex, Daniella and Cutter, Alexa and you, Epifania and Rudman, Ethel and Harold, Brock and Madison, and Tank and me. That's already too much to ask when you consider that Aiden will just be turning three, which means he will officially become Aiden 3.0. Sure, Luciana is doing her best to handle him, but from what I've seen, she has her hands full."

"Understatement of the year," Jennifer said. "Two months ago, my son mastered the art of running. Ever since, I think poor Luciana has lost ten pounds just trying to keep him from running into walls."

"Fine," I said. "I'll do it."

"Excuse me?" Jennifer said.

"I'll host Christmas Eve."

I watched Lisa finish off the rest of her martini in one fell swoop and then hold up her empty glass. She clearly caught someone's eye because she indicated that she needed another before she turned back to me. "Sorry, what was that?" she said. "*You* hosting Christmas Eve? Barbara, none of us have even seen your new apartment for God's sake. And you moved in four months ago."

"Then consider this your official invite," I said. "Because someone has to save the day, so it might as well be me. I do know how to throw a party, after all. And my new apartment is to die for. But what each of you also needs to consider is that this actually might be good for me."

"Good for you how?" Jennifer asked.

Time to come clean, I thought. *As much as a part of me likes to mess with these two, if only to see their reactions, not only are they my friends but also they have become an extension of my family. If I can't share how I'm feeling with them, then with whom?*

"I might have sold my old apartment and bought my new one for a reason," I said.

"What reason?" Jennifer asked.

Just tell them.

"A distraction."

"From what?"

"From missing my two daughters," I said. "It didn't work, because with them living on their own, I still miss them terribly. And now I have this monster of a show-place with expansive views of the park, and it does nothing for me. My life isn't the same without them living with me. There are times when it can be somewhat —dare I say the word—lonely."

"Lonely?" Jennifer said with concern. "Why haven't you told us this sooner?"

"I'm rather surprised I'm sharing it with you at all, but to hell with it. Apparently, even *I'm* capable of that emotion—who knew? But it's true, not that I want to dwell on *that* any further. If I host Christmas Eve, it would be good for everyone. It would take the pressure off Lisa; it would take the pressure off you, Jennifer; and it also would give me a fabulous reason to have my girls in my apartment at the same time, which hasn't been easy as of late. Each of them works long hours at Wenn. And with Daniella's relationship with Cutter still going strong, I'm lucky if I see *that* one at all these days."

"Barbara, if you're lonely, why don't you date?" Jennifer asked.

"Who in the hell is going to be interested in a sixty-year-old woman?" I said. "Even someone as fabulous as me?"

"Are you serious?" Lisa said. "Plenty, Barbara."

"Where are they?"

"These days, they're probably on a dating service like Elite Singles. You should try it. It's filled with professional men either looking for a chance at love or for a second chance at love. You can skim their profiles, look at their photos to see if you find any of them attractive, and maybe start dating again if you do."

"Well, look at you, Lisa," I said. "A married woman who happens to be unusually knowledgeable about an online dating service."

"Please," she said. "The only reason I know about it is because friends of mine have had terrific luck using it."

"Do you really believe I'm going to reduce myself to a dating service, Lisa? Really? Do you even know me?"

"It was just a thought."

"While I appreciate the concern, dating isn't in the

cards for me. I'm not sure I'll ever date again, let alone be in a relationship again. It's too much work, and it often leads to too much disappointment. Why would I ever put myself through it again?"

"Charles is happy with Rita, isn't he?" Jennifer asked. "Why couldn't you be happy with someone else again?"

"How dare you bring up my ex-husband and his ridiculously named wife when we should be talking about Christmas Eve."

"It was just an observation," she said.

"Look," I said after I finished my martini. "Why don't we glance over the menu, order dinner, and then discuss Christmas Eve? How does that sound? Because in case you haven't noticed, our waiter has been eyeballing us like a hawk, likely wondering if we're ever going to make our selections."

I picked up my menu, glanced inside, and then put it back down. "Caviar for the table to start?"

"Sounds good to me," Jennifer said.

"I'd love some caviar," Lisa said.

"Perfect. As for dinner, I'm having the Dover sole. I've had it here before, and the soy-lime emulsion is to die for."

"Salmon for me," Jennifer said.

"Glazed Maine lobster tail is on the menu," Lisa said. "So, clearly, that's what this Maine girl is having."

"How deliciously cliché of you. Now put your menus down so that poor man will know we're ready to order. And when we do, Jennifer and I will get another round of drinks, and we can start brainstorming about all things Christmas Eve."

"What about me?" Lisa said. "I'd like another cocktail."

"You're still on your second—a third will make you sloppy."

"I don't do sloppy, Barbara."

"Said the woman who writes about zombies with a certain hunger for human brains."

But when our waiter arrived, he was already carrying a silver tray with three martinis on it.

"What's this?" I asked as he removed our empty glasses before placing the fresh drinks in front of us. "We haven't ordered another round of cocktails yet."

"A gentleman at another table is buying this round," the waiter said.

"At which table?" I asked.

The man looked to his left and then smiled at me. "He's coming this way now. He said he wanted to say hello."

"Well shit," Jennifer said beneath her breath as she glanced across the room. "No way . . ."

"This was meant to be," Lisa said in a low voice as she followed Jennifer's gaze. "And by the way, who needs Elite Singles when the real thing turns up looking like that? He's smoking hot."

"What are you two talking about?" I asked as I looked over my shoulder.

And when I did? When I saw who was coming toward us, his smile as broad and as disarming as ever? I was looking straight at Marcus Koch, the only other man I'd been in love with.

Three years ago, I ended our relationship because his

globe-trotting lifestyle as a successful hedge fund manager left increasingly little time for us.

But here he was now, in a perfectly fitted black suit, his eyes as blue and as intense as I remembered them to be.

I didn't want to admit it, but my God did he ever look good . . .

TWO

BARBARA

"Marcus," I said when he stopped at the table. "What a surprise."

"Barbara," he said to me. "Jennifer. Lisa. It's good to see you. I was happy to notice you walk in—especially you, Barbara. I've missed you."

Before I could respond, Jennifer and Lisa said something about using the powder room and then they stood, leaving me alone with Marcus without any apparent care in the world.

I could have killed them at that moment, especially since they knew Marcus and I hadn't spoken to each other since I ended our relationship. What was I supposed to say to him now?

There's no need to be rude to him. Just get through it. Behave as if none of this matters to you.

"May I sit down?" he asked.

I looked around him.

"Aren't you with someone?"

"Just a business associate," he said. "Who understands why I wanted to come by and say hello."

"It's always business with you, Marcus," I said with a little shrug. "But, please, if you'd like, have a seat."

"About my business," he said after he sat opposite me. "Things have changed."

I couldn't give a damn about your business, Marcus, I thought. *It's your business that ended us.*

Be polite.

"Really?" I said. "What things?"

"I no longer have a reason to travel for work," he said. "I live here in the city now—permanently."

Permanently?

He looked me in the eyes. "I know I'm about to sideline you with what I have to say, so let me be quick before Jennifer and Lisa return."

Sideline me? I thought. *What is he talking about?*

Focus.

"Losing you forced me to reconsider my life," he said. "It's taken me three years to sort things out, but I've finally made the necessary changes to persuade you to give me a second chance."

"There will be no second chances," I said.

"Let me convince you why there should be," he said. "Over dinner."

"I'm not having dinner with you."

"You should, because I'm the same man you fell in love with, Barbara. The only difference is that I'm a hell of a lot more available to you now. I wanted you to know that."

I don't want to have this conversation, I thought. *Not now. Not ever. I can't let him hurt me again.*

"I'm not here by coincidence," he said.

"Clearly."

"You always work late," he said. "I wanted to catch you at work when you'd be alone, so I called you after hours. When you didn't answer, I called you at home, but instead I got your voice mail."

"How did you find me here, Marcus?"

"I called Daniella," he said. "We always had a good relationship. She told me that you'd be dining here tonight with Jennifer and Lisa, so here I am. Finally looking at you. I've missed you more than you know. I had to see you again."

My heart started to quicken when he said that, but before I became vulnerable to his advances, walls started to build around me in an effort to protect my heart.

"Look, Marcus, we gave it a go, didn't we?" I asked. "Unfortunately, it didn't work out. We're two very busy people who are probably best suited living alone."

"Do you really believe that?" he said.

Stay cool. Keep your head. Don't relent.

"I do."

"Why don't *I* believe you?"

Why don't I believe myself?

He pressed on.

"I made a mistake, and I want to apologize for it," he said. "I was traveling too much. I wasn't making enough time for us. Naturally you left me—and why not? I don't blame you. But I've changed all that—it's finished. With the exception of my office in Manhattan, I've shut down my offices all over the world. I've done the work and now I want to start seeing you again. Hell, I want you in my life and in my bed again. There is no one else like you. I was acutely aware of that when we first met at Sugarloaf, but I was stupid enough not to nurture it during the year I had it. Please believe me when I say the traveling part of my life is over. Please say you'll have dinner with me this week so that we can reconnect."

"I can't do that," I said.

"Why?"

"You want the truth?"

"I do."

"The question is whether you can handle it."

"I can handle it."

"I've loved only two men in my life, Marcus—you and my ex-husband. Each of you hurt me in different ways. What you must know after spending a year with me is that I will not allow that to happen again. I'm simply not that person. Never have been, never will be."

"Minds can be changed."

"Mine can't. Not when it comes to this."

"Tell me you don't feel something for me."

"I will always think of you with fondness, Marcus—but that's as far as it goes." I looked at my watch. "Now look, as you pointed out, Jennifer and Lisa will be back soon, and I do not want them to be part of this conversation. It was good seeing you, but I'm afraid I have to ask you to leave. I hope you'll respect my reasons why."

"I'm not giving up," he said as he stood. "We're right for each other. You know it, and I know it. I've seen no one since you." He leaned toward me and lowered his voice so that those around us couldn't hear him. "Why? It's because I can't get you out of my fucking head."

The moment he dipped toward me, I could smell a whiff of the cologne he was wearing. It was Chanel's Allure Homme Édition Blanche. Of course it was. He knew how much I adored Chanel.

He thought of everything before he came here tonight, I thought. *And what am I to make of that?*

Nothing.

So it's that easy to dispense with him?

It needs to be.

"Marcus, it's time for you to get me out of your head." I lifted the martini he sent over and took a sip of it. "Belvedere," I said. "You remembered."

"I've never forgotten."

Why does he have to be so goddamned handsome? And why do I have to remember what it was like to make love to him? What is wrong with me? He's a mere attraction. I'm better than this.

Are you?

Of course I am.

I wonder if that's true?

"Go," I said when I saw Jennifer and Lisa approach the table. "There are the girls now."

"I'll be in touch," he said before he left.

"Marcus, please don't."

"Tonight your dinner is on me," he said and then he was gone just as Jennifer and Lisa arrived.

"WHAT IN THE fresh hell was that?" Jennifer asked as she sat down.

"And what are the odds of him being here tonight considering all the restaurants this city has to offer?" Lisa said as she reclaimed her seat. "That was either fate, coincidence, or something else."

"I'd rather not discuss it," I said, meaning it. I felt unusually rattled. Seeing Marcus again had shaken me.

And that's the last thing I'm going to show these two.

So I reached for my martini and took another sip to calm my nerves.

"Your hand is trembling," Jennifer said. "What did he say to you?"

"I'd really prefer it if we—"

"We're your *friends*," she interrupted. "And the only time I've seen you behave like this is the night you decided to leave him."

"Otherwise known as the night I got drunk and pitched into your Christmas tree?"

"That would be the night, Barbara."

"How kind of you to bring it up now."

"The kindness I'm offering is my friendship. Now what did he say? Is it a coincidence that he's here? Because I'm with Lisa—I don't think it is."

There was no getting away from their questions, so I gave in to them.

"It wasn't a coincidence." I sighed.

Before they could hammer me with questions, I told them everything that had transpired between Marcus and me, if only to be done with it. I told them why he was here, how he found me here, what he said to me, what I said to him—all of it. In silence, they listened until I said, "And that's the end of it."

"Sounds like that's the beginning of it, if you ask me," Lisa said.

"But that's the thing, my dear—I asked you nothing."

"Fine. Then strike the last part of that sentence, because this sounds like the beginning of something. Jennifer?"

"Likely," she said. She turned to me. "You made him sound so alpha. Was he?"

"He was."

"If that's the case, he probably isn't going to give up easily, Barbara."

"I understand that."

"How are you going to keep him at bay?"

"By ignoring him. He'll eventually tire of that and move on. Every man has their breaking point. He'll soon meet his."

"But if he changed his life—and especially for you, no less—why not entertain the idea of seeing him again, even if it is just for dinner?" Lisa asked. "You two were wonderful together. And Marcus is a nice man. He's also hot—let's not forget that."

Before I could reply, Jennifer answered for me.

"He broke her heart, Lisa," she said as the caviar course arrived. "Despite how promising this seems, she's not willing to risk it again."

"You think this sounds promising?" I asked her.

"Let's put it this way," Jennifer said as she leaned forward and placed caviar and a dollop of crème fraîche on top of a blini. "I think you're about to find out . . ."

THREE

MARCUS

"By the look on your face, that didn't go so well."

I had rejoined my longtime best friend and business partner, Jonathan Stack, at our table, which was across the room from where Barbara, Jennifer, and Lisa were sitting.

I noted the fresh glass of scotch in front of me, picked it up, lifted it to him in a show of thanks, and then took a long pull from it as I looked over at Barbara, whose back was to me.

"Actually, better than I expected," I said. "When I asked if I could sit down, she agreed. I wasn't anticipating that."

"Neither was I. What did she have to say?"

I gave him the rundown. Characteristic of Jon, who was the vice president and portfolio manager of the newly renamed Koch Capital Advisors, a company I started twenty years ago as Koch International Management, he listened quietly and spoke only when I was finished.

"Think she'll come around?" he asked.

I shrugged. "You've met Barbara. You know how she is."

"Strong-willed to the bone."

"One of the things I love most about her."

"But maybe not so much in this situation . . ."

"Not really. Winning her back will be worth the fight. I screwed up when it came to us. I blew it. I don't expect her to make things easy for me. If this is going to happen—if she's going to agree to take me back into her life—I'm going to have to fight for it and earn it, which is only fair. But I plan on doing it."

"She pretty much just shut you down, buddy."

"Yeah, well, she also tried to do that when we first met at Sugarloaf. Didn't work so well for her then, did it?"

It didn't.

As I looked at Barbara, I recalled the first day we met. We'd been waiting in line at the ski lift when I decided I had to get a better look at the woman standing at my back, boldly stating in a raised voice that she was about to crush it on the slopes, even though the wary conversations from those around her suggested she'd never skied before.

I'd revisited that memory so often, it had become something like a movie I could play in my head.

And so I allowed it to run, skipping our initial introductions and going straight to the moment Barbara lost control on the slopes, slammed into me—and then fell on top of me, our arms and legs entwined. Our faces had been so close, we could have kissed.

———

"I'M SO SORRY," *she said as she looked down at me.* "My God—how awful of me."

"Is it?" I asked with a grin. "I mean, if two people were going to make a mess of it on a mountainside, at least we did it with style. Don't you think?"

Instead of answering, she asked if she'd hurt me.

"I'm flat on my back with a beautiful woman on top of me," I said. "Believe me, I'm not feeling any pain."

"And how am I to respond to that?"

"Maybe with a smile?"

"Please. People are watching. Paparazzi might be taking our photographs. We must untangle ourselves."

"Paparazzi," I said. "Should I know you?"

"I'm a legend."

"Well, my mysterious legend, I think that getting out of this situation is going to be a bit of a challenge. Your right leg is hooked around my left knee in a weird kind of way. And I think that one of your bootstraps has somehow locked itself onto one of mine. Are you able to remove it?"

"Well, of course I can. I'm fully capable of any task. Just maneuver your body to the left."

"I can't," I said. "You've got me pinned. And since you do, maybe we should just stay like this for a while and get to know each other better."

"I hardly see that happening."

"You're a handful," I said. "Not that I mind."

"You have no idea." She raised an eyebrow. "And by the way, that should terrify you."

"And yet somehow it doesn't."

"You should know I eat ice cubes for lunch," she said. "Consider that."

"And yet you feel so warm against me. I wonder why that is?"

"If I feel warm against you, it's only because I just tumbled down a goddamned mountain."

"Hmm," I said, looking her in the eyes. "Why don't I believe that?"

Her only response was to stare at me.

"Look, Barbara," I said after a member of her group started to unlock our boots. "Since you nearly just took my life, you now must have a drink with me, if only to make amends. Meet me at the lodge tonight. Don't say no. It's just one drink."

"Oh look—the oldest line in the book! And what if I'm married? Have you considered that?"

"Are you?"

"Actually, I'm not."

"Divorced?"

"I hardly share my personal life with strangers."

"So you are divorced. Been through one myself. I didn't like it when I caught my wife cheating on me."

When I said that, I saw something soften in her expression. For an instant, she seemed to assess me with new eyes.

"Just one drink—I promise," I said. "I'm here alone. My children are with their mother, and it would be nice to spend some time with someone interesting for once."

"How do you know that I'm interesting? What if I'm dull and disappointing? What if I'm this kind of horror show off the slopes?"

"Yeah, I kind of doubt that."

"Well, at least you're intuitive," she said.

"I read people quickly."

"Is that so?"

"Actually, it is. I wouldn't have asked you for that drink if I thought it was going to be a waste of my time. Not in me."

"There," a young muscular man said when he released whatever parts of our boots were hooked together. "You're free."

In one swift, fluid motion, I swept one foot beneath me, pressed down hard on it, and lifted Barbara off my body as I stood.

"Are you all right?" I asked her. "Nothing sprained or broken?"

"I'm as healthy as Chanel's bottom line."

"You do have a way with words," I said.

"You have no idea how I wield my words, Mr. Koch."

"Please, since you have, after all, been on top of me, at the very least call me by my first name. In case you've forgotten, it's Marcus."

"Fine then—Marcus. Thank you for cushioning my fall."

"Is that what you call it?" Before she could speak, I raised my hand. "I'm joking," I said. "I'm just glad I was there to help stop you, because you really could have hurt yourself. It's still a long way to the bottom of the mountain, so be careful, OK?"

"After that scene, I'll walk down this damned mountain if I have to."

"And yet why do I feel as if you're about to put those

skis on again and give it another go? I don't know you, Barbara, but I can already tell you're no quitter. So see you at the bar in the lodge at eight?"

"I never agreed to that."

"You'll be there," I said as I lowered my goggles over my eyes. "I know you will. You have to come. We both know it."

"How utterly confident of you."

"That's the thing," I said. "I am confident but not arrogant. I just want to share a drink with you—and after that blunder, you owe me that. I'll see you tonight."

"You must know that I am not to be had for the mere price of a mountain collision," she said.

———

BUT LATER THAT NIGHT, with her family and friends in tow, she had shown up at the bar, which had been the beginning of us. And now here I sat sipping scotch with the woman I still loved no more than thirty feet away from me. Her back to me as if I didn't exist. As if I wasn't here. No longer could I touch her like I used to, and if that wasn't hell, I wasn't sure what was. Because touching her? Kissing her? Making love to her?

I missed all of it to my core.

"What's on your mind, buddy?" Jon asked me.

"Life," I said with resolve as I looked across the room at Barbara. "And how mine is about to change for the better."

FOUR

BARBARA

"If Marcus plans to pursue you, you have to know your life is about to change," Lisa said as our waiter approached with our meals. "And hopefully for the better."

"I'm done talking about this," I said with steel in my voice. "Especially in public. So stop it. I'm over it."

"But don't you think we *should* talk about it?" she asked as she leaned toward me. "I mean, he's right over there—literally watching you."

"Which is *exactly* what I needed to know, Lisa. Thank you for that."

"I'm only trying to help."

"Well, you aren't." I looked at Jennifer, who naturally was stealing sidelong glances at Marcus. I cleared my throat so sharply that she turned to me, wide-eyed. "Would you please kick your friend in the ass for me?" I asked. "I'd do it, but my shoes are new, and I'd rather not bloody them."

"Jesus," Lisa said. "That's harsh."

"Harsh?" I said with a little laugh. "Please. This from the woman whose zombies eat children for breakfast."

"Only the naughty ones."

"Ladies," our waiter said as he arrived at our table.

The moment we heard his voice, each of us got in line and forced a smile on our faces as he served us. When he was finished, we thanked him. I admired each dish and thought that while everything certainly looked delicious, I was having none of it.

My appetite was gone. With Marcus sitting so close—and literally watching me, as Lisa kindly pointed out—I just wanted to go home and go to bed. The girls and I could discuss Christmas in the morning.

I was about to take a final sip of my martini and suggest that we leave when I was derailed by that lovely voice in the back of my head—the one whose tone often felt like a slap from a stranger.

Since when does anyone chase you out of a restaurant —or anywhere else, for that matter? You're Barbara Blackwell, for God's sake. My suggestion is that you get a grip, because if Marcus sees you leave after your talk with him? And before you've even touched your food? He's going to know he's gotten under your skin, he's going to sense your vulnerability—and the lot of it will give him hope for a second chance with you.

It won't, I thought. *It can't.*

But it will.

And how do you know that?

Marcus may have agreed to let you go once, but look at what he's done in the meantime to get you back. He said he's changed his life for you. He said he's put in the work.

He's even cut out the travel. And now that he's free to be laser-focused on you, he's roared back into your life with plenty of expectations. Just try dodging him now. As kind as he is, he's also every bit as strong-willed as you. If you think for one moment that he's going to go quietly into the night, you are dead wrong.

"Barbara?" Jennifer said to me. "Are you all right? Your fish is getting cold."

He's watching you. Don't let him get to you. Eat.

"I was simply allowing it to cool," I said as I took a bite of the fish. "And look at that—perfection."

"How about if we talk about Christmas in the morning?" Jennifer asked. "Right now doesn't seem to be the best time."

"As much as I wanted this hammered down tonight, I agree," Lisa said. "We need to be focused. When works best for you, Barbara?"

"I have a busy day tomorrow, so it will have to be before my first meeting. How about six?"

"I'll be there," Jennifer said.

"Same," Lisa said as she picked at her lobster. "But we're going to have to come up with something fast, because Ethel is expecting an answer from me sooner rather than later. If I disappoint her, God knows what kind of bullshit she'll pull."

"We'll figure it out," Jennifer said.

"That's the thing about us," I said to them. "We always do."

WHEN WE FINISHED OUR MEAL, it was approaching nine p.m., the restaurant was hopping, and a mere glance at Jennifer and Lisa confirmed what I already knew—they kept looking across the room at Marcus.

"So he's still here," I said to them. It wasn't a question —it was an observation.

"He's still here," Jennifer said.

"It looks as if he's sipping a glass of bourbon or some-thing," Lisa said.

"And lying in wait for me?"

I didn't give them time to answer.

"Tell me how to get out of here without causing a scene."

"First of all, Marcus is not going to cause a scene," Jennifer said. "He's a gentleman. He's aware that people know you in this city. He also knows the same is true for Lisa and me."

"Lisa?" I said. "How is she known in this city?"

"She's a best-selling novelist, Barbara."

"Right," I said. "Right, right. Why do I always forget that?"

"Because you have selective dementia," Lisa said.

I turned to her.

"I'm sorry, but what is your name again?"

She smiled sweetly at me. "Marcus."

"You're a horrible person."

Jennifer tapped her finger on the table. "Anyway, he's not going to embarrass anyone," she said. "I think the only reason he's still here is because he's happy to see you. If he wants you back in his life—"

"Not happening."

She sighed. "Regardless, if he wants you back in his life, he's no fool. He knows he's going to have to be on his best behavior and wait you out while he tries to wear you down. You know, with flowers or something. Anything to get you to have dinner with him so that he can reason with you. At least that's how I see it. Lisa?"

"He's a romantic," she said. "And he's in love with you. He's not going to do anything to jeopardize what he wants most from you—a second chance."

"Or to get me into his bed again."

"Excuse me?" Jennifer said.

I shrugged. "*He's* the one who said it."

"When?"

"Just a moment ago. You know, when you two left me alone with him."

"Well shit, if he also wants that—which of course he does—don't worry about him," Jennifer said. "Let me pay the bill, and we'll leave. If he says good night to you on our way out, simply nod and keep moving."

"Just so you know, he said *he's* going to pay the bill."

"Not if I get ahead of him with our waiter."

"What am I to do if he follows us outside?"

"He's not going to do that," she said. "But to ease your mind, let me call Cutter and ask him to wait for us at the entrance. When he arrives, I'll have him send me a text. Then we'll leave the restaurant and step into the car without having to wait on the sidewalk."

"How very 007 of you," I said.

"You know," Lisa said as Jennifer removed her cell

from her purse and called Cutter, "thirty years ago, you would have made one hell of a Bond girl."

I turned to her with a raised eyebrow. "Thirty years ago? Seriously? I could pull that off now."

"Of course you could," she said. "I mean, these days? CGI can do *anything*."

"Are you suggesting I need to be digitally enhanced?"

"Not when it comes to Marcus, I'm not."

Jennifer put her phone down on the table. "Are you two about finished?" she asked.

"Darling, we're just getting started," I said.

"No, you're not. Cutter will be here in five."

And he was.

When Jennifer received his text, she nodded at our waiter before turning her attention back to me.

"You've got this," she said.

"I know I do," I said. "It's just that all of this is so unexpected."

"Not for him it isn't—he's been planning this day for years."

"Ladies?" our waiter said when he approached our table.

"The check, please," Jennifer said.

"The check has already been settled, Mrs. Wenn," he said. "Mr. Koch sends his regards."

Jennifer looked over at me.

"Just let it go," I said. "I'd rather leave than fight over a check he never should have paid for." I looked up at the waiter. "Did he at least tip you well?"

"He tipped me extremely well," the man said.

Of course he did, I thought. *That's who Marcus is.*

"We should leave," I said when the waiter stepped away. "How are we doing this?"

"I'll lead the way," Jennifer said. "Then you, then Lisa. When we walk past him, you'll be sandwiched between us when we go to retrieve our coats."

"We'll be your force field," Lisa said.

When I turned to her, she shot me a look of concern.

"Remind me to put you in my will," I said. "Because a force field is exactly what I need right now."

WHEN WE STOOD TO LEAVE, I followed Jennifer's lead.

When we had reclaimed our clutches from the backs of our chairs, I took a breath to calm my nerves and then followed Jennifer as she stepped past a host of tables on our left and right and moved toward the coat check at the front entrance. The sound of Lisa's heels clicking behind me gave me an unexpected sense of solace.

If this was going to happen to me tonight, at least I have these two with me, I thought. *Yes, we enjoy our bitchy little asides with one another, but at this point, each of us knows those exchanges are only ever meant to be fun. Thank God they appreciate them as much as I do.*

As we approached Marcus's table, my stomach sank when I saw him stand to face us.

He's going to say something to you, I thought. *Be prepared for it.*

"Jennifer," Marcus said as we drew closer to him.

"Thank you for dinner, Marcus," she said without pausing. "It was lovely."

"I'm glad you enjoyed it." As she walked past him, he looked straight at me, his eyes so blue and his lips so full, they evoked within me a sudden feeling of loss, heartbreak, and longing.

Just get me through this.

To my surprise, Marcus said nothing as I moved past him. Instead, he had something more powerful in mind—he lowered his hand and intentionally brushed the back of it against mine. Feeling the warmth of his skin after so many years was almost too much. I willed myself not to react to it, but the reality was that his touch was like a fire I never expected to feel again.

Why is he doing this? I wondered as we approached the coat check. *I ended our relationship. He knows where I stand when it comes to us—I just told him again this evening. We're finished!*

But as I was about to learn over the coming days and weeks, Marcus Koch couldn't disagree more.

FIVE

BARBARA

After a restless night that offered zero sleep, I pulled myself together the following morning, chose a black Chanel suit to match my mood, took a taxi to Wenn, and was seated at my desk when Jennifer and Lisa arrived at six to discuss Christmas Eve.

"How are you?" Jennifer asked when she and Lisa entered my office. "I've been thinking of you."

"So have I," Lisa said. "What happened to you yesterday came out of nowhere."

"To say the least," I said, motioning to the two chairs on the opposite side of my desk. "Have a seat."

"Have you heard anything else from Marcus?" Jennifer asked as she and Lisa sat down.

"No, but I'm sure I will in time."

"How are you going to handle him?"

"As I said yesterday, I'm going to ignore him. He'll have none of that at first, but eventually he'll grow tired of my cold shoulder and move on with his life."

"But he said he's still in love with you," Lisa said.

"And he's made changes in his life so that he can devote more time to you. How can you ignore that? He tracked you down last night because he knows he's finally at a point where he can fully commit to you."

"And it took him three years to do so?" I asked. "The sheer motivation of it all is staggering."

"Actually, the timing sounds about right," Jennifer said. "Since Koch International Management had offices and hundreds of employees all over the world, there's no question it could have taken him that long to shut things down. You know that as well as I do."

"And yet here I sit wanting to discuss none of it," I said. "This meeting is supposed to be about Christmas Eve, which is only three weeks away. If I'm going to host it—which I'm perfectly happy to do—we need to start discussing everything from the food to the decor to the invitations to the best way to handle Ethel and Aiden."

"Barbara, the only reason Lisa and I are discussing Marcus is because we want nothing but the best for you," Jennifer said. "Marcus isn't just a good man—he also happens to be the perfect man for you. We've all witnessed the chemistry you share with him. Yes, when you were together, he made the mistake of not spending enough time with you, but doesn't it speak volumes about him that he's fixed that?"

"How am I to know that he's fixed anything?"

"You Google it," Lisa said. "As I did last night. According to the articles I read in the *Times* and the *Wall Street Journal*, Koch International Management has since become Koch Capital Advisors. Why? Because Marcus was telling the truth last night—he no longer has offices abroad. Due to all kinds of legal and contractual reasons, it took him three years to dismantle them, but he's done it. And do you want to know what I find interesting?"

"Not really."

"I'm still going to tell you," she said. "A week ago, he closed his last international office in Paris. And last night, he wasted no time in hunting you down at Le Bernadin. He's that serious, Barbara."

"And once again, I'm here to tell you I've moved on," I said. "Now look, girls—I appreciate your enthusiasm, but I just don't share it. As much as I hate to admit it, Jennifer got it right last night—by focusing more on his work than on our relationship, Marcus did hurt me. Will he make that mistake again? I'm not willing to find out, so that's the end of it."

The disappointment on their faces was as clear as my resolve. In an effort to move forward, I straightened in my chair and looked at Jennifer.

"First, I want to discuss what I should have mentioned yesterday."

"What's that?" she asked.

"Your appointment with your gynecologist. I was so overwhelmed yesterday, I forgot you were seeing her at noon. I apologize for that. What did she say?"

She smiled at me.

"That I'm an excellent candidate for IVF."

"Oh thank goodness," I said.

"It's literally the best news ever," Lisa said.

I turned to her.

"You already know?" I asked.

"After Alex, I was the second to find out."

"If that's the case, you can forget what I said last night about adding you to my will."

"Lady, I never counted on it, so we're good."

"Anyway," Jennifer said. "Once I found out, I discussed it with Alex, and we've decided to go for it. We want another child. As each of you know, we've been trying for months to get pregnant. On the one hand, that's been a lot of fun, but on the other hand, it's also been frustrating." She looked at each of us. "I'm tired of being a disappointment."

"You are no disappointment," Lisa said.

I pointed my finger at her.

"You aren't."

"Well, I feel like one," she said. "We got lucky with Aiden, but he's three now. I need to get pregnant next year because Alex and I want Aiden to be as close in age to his future sibling as possible. This might be the answer."

"When do you think you'll start?" I asked.

"After the New Year."

"Does your doctor have any idea how long it will take?"

"Apparently, that depends on way too many factors," Jennifer said. "But I did press her on the issue."

"What did she say?"

"That it's a process," she said. "And a long one with many important steps. If you want, we can discuss what those are later, but in the end, she said that one cycle of IVF takes about two months to produce an embryo."

"So you could be pregnant by spring?" Lisa asked.

"It's a possibility," Jennifer said.

"May it work," I said. "And thank you for telling me, Jennifer. I'm sorry I didn't ask you about it yesterday."

"You had your reasons," she said.

I raised my eyebrows.

"To say the least," I said. "But let's not go there again. We're here to discuss the party. Shall we?"

"Let's do it," Jennifer said.

"Good." I turned to Lisa. "I've given Ethel some thought."

"I'm sorry," she said. "Did you have to see your own doctor afterward?"

"Not at all, and I'll tell you why. I think she'll be mindful of her behavior for two reasons—she'll be a guest in my home, which should terrify her, and she'll also know that her son and daughter-in-law will be watching her every move. Unless I'm completely wrong about her, that alone should be enough to keep her in check at the party. As for them staying at your house, my advice is for you to suck it up and try your best to get through it."

"Oh thanks," Lisa said.

"We live in New York City," I said to her. "Be creative, for God's sake. Since they've never been to Manhattan, simply stuff every day with so many things for them to see and do, Ethel will be too distracted and entertained to cause trouble."

"She'll find a way," Lisa said. "It's who she is."

"Then poison her and be finished with her for good."

"I'm not above it, Barbara."

"Clearly you aren't, darling—your books say it all."

"Hilarious."

I looked at Jennifer.

"As for Aiden, whenever he's around the people he loves the most, he can become excitable. We need to be prepared for that. Also, these gatherings tend to go deep into the night. At some point, he'll want to take a nap, so I'll make sure one of my bedrooms is made childproof for him. Do you think Luciana should be there to tend to him?"

"Absolutely," she said. "And since we'll all be dressed to the nines, I'll make sure to buy her a beautiful dress so that she feels less like a nanny and more like a member of the family, which she is."

"Perfect."

At that moment, Alex appeared in my doorway carrying what had to be at least two dozen red roses in red tissue paper. He was wearing a navy blue business suit, his handsome face was peppered with dark stubble, and his hair—freshly cut by Bernie last week—was styled with a hard part on the right.

"Good morning, everyone," he said.

I smiled at Jennifer. "Looks like somebody is getting roses," I said. "*J'adore* it."

"Well shit," Alex said. "Now I'm going to look bad."

"I'm not following," I said.

"That's because these roses aren't for Jennifer, Barbara. They're for you."

"For me?"

"They're from Marcus."

"Marcus?" I said. "But why do you have them?"

"Because I just spent the last thirty minutes with him," he said.

As surprised as I was, I refused to show it. Instead, I kept my expression stoic. Neutral.

"Where?"

"In my office. This morning, he sent me a text asking if I had time to meet with him. I did, so I invited him to drop by." He lifted the bouquet of roses. "He asked me to give you these."

"He couldn't do that himself?"

"Baby steps, Barbara. He knows you don't want to see him just yet, but he still wanted you to have them." After he moved into the room and gave Jennifer a quick kiss on the lips, he looked at me. "There's a card," he said. "You should read it."

"Actually, I feel like burning the lot of it, but that would be a waste, wouldn't it?" When I saw the disappointment on his face, I could only wish all of them understood why I wanted nothing to do with Marcus Koch.

Why don't they understand how much he hurt me? I thought. *And how much Charles hurt me? To hell with men. I'm not going there again.*

"If you would do me a favor and give the roses to Ann, I'd appreciate it, Alex. As for the card, just throw it away. I'm sorry he bothered you."

"He didn't bother me, Barbara," he said. "He just he needed someone to talk with—specifically someone who knows and understands you well."

"But that's the thing," I said. "Nobody *really* knows me, Alex. I'm an enigma wrapped in a riddle."

"You like to think you are, but that's not exactly true," he said. "At least not when it comes to me. I've known you since I was a boy. I remember when you first became friends with my mother and then when you started working for my father. Years later, you were the one who took me under your wing when my father ended their lives. You were the one who supported me when the board urged me to take the reins at Wenn. You were the one who was there for me when that truck slammed into Diana's car and killed her. I know you better than most, Barbara."

He never talked about his parents or his first wife. That he just did so startled me.

What did Marcus say to him?

"Look," he said. "It's not like me to get involved in anyone's personal life—especially their love life. But after listening to Marcus? I believe him. He knows he screwed up by not spending more time with you. Did he know you were upset with him because of that? No, he didn't, but he sure as hell regrets it now. His understanding was that you were like him. He thought you also wanted to have it all—work *and* a relationship. And that's why he was stunned when you broke up with him on Christmas Eve. He's still in love with you, Barbara. He wants you back. Do you have any idea what he's done with his business since you dropped him? Because if you don't, you need to know. It speaks volumes about how serious he is to fix things with you."

"Not that it matters, but he mentioned something about it last night," I said. "A few moments ago, Lisa also gave me some additional insights."

"Good, then you know that for Marcus, you're the one who comes first now."

"But how do I really know that? How can I even *believe* that?"

"Are you calling him a liar?"

"No, because that wouldn't be true. What I *am* saying is that Marcus is a successful businessman who likely will come to resent me when the money from his international operations stops coming in."

"Don't you think he's already taken that into account?" Alex asked.

"Frankly, I don't know what is going through that man's head."

"Then let me enlighten you."

"Please, don't."

"Actually, I think I should, because I happen to love you—even when you're being this bullheaded."

"Bullheaded?"

"Would you please just listen to me?"

If I don't listen to him now, I'll only be forced to do so later. So let him talk.

"Go ahead," I said.

"Of course Marcus knows he's going to lose hundreds of millions by shutting down his international offices," Alex said. "But you already know that. You also know he had three years to change his mind about you, but he didn't. Instead, he went forward with his plans to win you back because you mean more to him than money."

And then Alex shrugged.

"I liked Marcus when you two were first together, Barbara, but after talking with him this morning? I like him even more. What I hope is that you'll have dinner with him and hear him out."

"Are we finished?" I asked.

"I tried," Alex said. Looking discouraged, he motioned toward Jennifer and Lisa. "I think we all have. The final decision is yours, Barbara."

"It always has been." The moment I said that, I know it sounded cold, so I immediately changed my tone. "But that doesn't mean I don't appreciate all of you and your concern. Just know that I'm at a very good place in my life right now. I have a new apartment, Chanel's fall line continues to give me life, and I—"

"Last night, you told Lisa and me that you're lonely," Jennifer said.

"A momentary blip."

"Or a truth you won't recognize now?"

"The former."

"But how do you know that?"

"Because I'm Blackwell," I said. "I can fix anything."

"Then fix your relationship with Marcus," Alex said after he tossed the roses onto a side table. "Because if you are lonely, Barbara? In my opinion, he's your best bet to remedy that."

SIX

BARBARA

When Alex left my office, Jennifer and Lisa joined him, promising they'd be in touch soon to discuss plans for Christmas Eve. I waited for Jennifer to close the door behind her before I fished for a piece of ice in a nearby glass, popped it into my mouth, and crunched down so hard on it, I smashed it into bits.

And naturally, because the universe was clearly conspiring against me this week, doing so wasn't nearly as satisfying as it should have been.

So now he's reached out to Alex, I thought as I looked over at the bouquet of roses. *But to what end? Marcus knows how much Charles's affair devastated me. He knows how difficult it was for me to trust again—but I did with him. Marcus convinced me that he was somehow different from other men, and I believed him. Unlike Charles, he didn't cheat on me with another woman, but one's work can be a mistress, can't it? It can be the one thing you'd rather spend time with than the woman you claim to love, which is exactly why I chose to leave him.*

And now he wants me back. Worse, my closest friends think I should give him another chance.

In my heart, I knew they were wrong—but with a catch. Jennifer and Lisa were two die-hard romantics. As such, their opinions needed to be dismissed. What gave me pause is that Alex had taken the time to meet with Marcus, and now, after their conversation, he was siding with him.

I glanced at the roses Alex had left on the side table and remembered all the times Marcus had sent me similar bouquets while he was away on business.

In the beginning, I had loved receiving flowers from him. After all, we were newly in love. But as the months passed and we saw less and less of each other, I began to resent them because they started to look more like guilt to me.

A fast and easy way for Marcus to try to remain in my heart.

I got up from my desk and turned to look out the windows overlooking Fifth Avenue. It was the first week of December, but with the exception of the decorative storefronts, you'd barely know it. The temperatures were moderate, we'd yet to have snow—

Read the card.

I looked over my shoulder at the roses.

Should I read it? Should I see what he has to say to me? Or does it even matter?

To a point, I decided it did, if only because I was curious to see how he felt he was going to fix what couldn't be fixed.

Before I could look, a knock came at my office door.

"Mom?"

Daniella, I thought. *The one who told Marcus where I was last night.*

I sat down at my desk, fingered a strand of hair away from my forehead, and chose to wait for a second knock to come. A moment later, it did.

"Mom, are you there?"

"I'm here, Daniella."

When she opened the door and entered the room, I noted that she was wearing a turtleneck rib-knit sweater in black, a matching leather skirt that came just to her knee, and a pair of tribute patent platform sandals—all by Theory. For the past several months, she'd been the director of trend at Wenn Fashion, and even though I was disappointed with her for mainlining Marcus back into my life, I nevertheless thought she looked lovely today.

"Are you angry with me?" she asked.

"Why don't you close the door behind you, have a seat, and we'll discuss the reasons you decided to betray me."

When I said that, her eyes widened as she closed the door.

"*Betray* you?" she said. "What are you talking about?"

"When you told Marcus where I'd be last night, that's exactly what you did. And you know it."

She took the seat opposite me.

"Mom, betraying you is the last thing I'd ever do," she said.

"And yet here we sit in a room clouded with betrayal."

"Don't be dramatic."

"If you don't want the drama, don't mess with the tattered shreds of my love life."

"Do you even want a love life?"

"You already know the answer to that question."

"We've only discussed that twice," she said. "First, when you decided to divorce Dad—"

"For cheating on me."

"That's right. And second, when you broke up with Marcus. But that was three years ago. When we talked about it, everything you told Alexa and me was said in the heat of the moment. You said you were through with men. I respected that then, but I also know that time can change minds."

I leaned forward in my seat.

"What I want to know is why everyone is trying to change mine. Do none of you know me?"

She crossed her legs at the knee and leveled me with a glance.

"Do you really want to go there?" she asked.

"Before you do, let me suggest this, Daniella—call PETA now. Because if you do go there, you're only going to be beating a dead horse."

"No, I'm not."

"Yes, you are. And I have a meeting in thirty minutes. Now is not the time to psychoanalyze your mother."

"There never will be a good time," she said. "So let me just leave you with this—you changed when Dad cheated on you."

"You think?"

"You became harder," she said. "Bitter—and I get that. Why wouldn't you be bitter? Or angry? Or hurt? It didn't happen all at once, but over time your skin became so thick, it was as if you chose to make it impenetrable. Alexa and I were aware of it. She and I even talked about it. I'm sure others did as well."

"What is your point, Daniella?"

"My point is that when you met Marcus, the chance you took on him made you lighter. Happier. You were in love again, and it showed. That's all any of us want for you, Mom. And yes, when he called me yesterday, that's the reason I told him where you were, but only after he and I had one hell of a discussion."

"What discussion?"

"When I asked what his intentions were, he told me everything he's been doing in an effort to win you back. When I asked him why he didn't tell you about that sooner, he said it was because he knew you wouldn't believe him until the work was done. And he's right—you wouldn't have believed him. But he's done it because he's that serious about having you back in his life."

"So I keep hearing, and yet look at me—I have no interest."

"Because you're afraid of being hurt again?"

"Wouldn't you be?"

She shook her head.

"Marcus isn't Dad, Mom. He didn't cheat on you like Dad did. He made a mistake, and he has owned that mistake. Has Dad ever owned what he did to you? No, he hasn't, but Marcus has, and that difference alone is so major, it should tell you to take this situation seriously."

She looked over at the roses on the table next to her.

"Are those from Marcus?"

"In fact, they are."

"I see a card—what does it say?"

"I have no idea."

"Don't you want to know?"

"Daniella, please stop pressing me," I said as I stood. She moved to speak, but I held up my hand. "We'll be having Christmas Eve at my apartment this year," I said.

That surprised her.

"We will?"

"We will. And just so you know, my focus and energy is going to be spent on that."

"And not on a man?"

"Exactly."

"We'll see what Marcus has to say about that," she said as she stood. "Because he's gone to way too much trouble to just walk away from you now."

"I can handle him."

"That's the thing," she said as she plucked the card from the bouquet and read it. For a moment, her eyes became bright with tears, which she quickly blinked away.

What in the hell does that card say?

I watched her put the card back before she turned to me.

"You're not going to be able to handle him."

"The hell I'm not."

"You aren't. You're going to lose, but the good news is that when you do lose, you're also going to win."

"What are you talking about?"

She looked at me for a long, lingering moment before she walked over to the door to let herself out.

"You'll see," she said.

Without saying another word, my once immature and often combative daughter left my office without any of her usual theatrics. At last, likely because of her new responsibilities at Wenn, she was growing up. Finally, she was behaving like an adult. And now?

When the door clicked shut behind her, now that she was gone, clearly knowing that no matter how much I wanted to dismiss our conversation, I had no choice but to face it.

I looked over at the bouquet of roses, and this time, without hesitation, I walked over and removed the card. I saw Marcus's familiar masculine handwriting and then I read what he'd written, well aware that my hand was trembling as I did so.

I'm in love with you, Barbara. Give me a second chance.

But to what end? I wondered. *None of my friends or my daughters will ever know the true depths of just how much you hurt me because I refuse to look weak to them. When I divorced Charles, I came out of that marriage a stronger woman. I was able to leave you because leaving Charles gave me the strength to do so. And now, after three years, you suddenly want me back?*

I shook my head at the card before I tore it in half.

"I can't do it, Marcus," I said aloud. "Because if I do? If I'm stupid enough to make that mistake? You could devastate me again—and that's a risk I'm not willing to take."

SEVEN

MARCUS

When I left Alex at Wenn, he said he'd send me a text after he gave Barbara the roses.

"You're going to want to know how she reacted to them," he'd said.

And he was right.

An hour after I returned to my office at Koch Capital Advisors, which was located high above Fifth and Fifty-First Streets in a gleaming high-rise, he followed through.

With a ding, my phone lit up on my desk. I looked over at it, reached for it, and read his text.

It didn't go well, Alex wrote. In fact, if I'm being honest, I think she's either going to throw the roses away or give them to someone else. I'm sorry, Marcus—but if I were you, I wouldn't give up. Wear her down. Let me know if you need anything more from me.

None of what I read concerned me because none of it surprised me. I knew there was no way that a few dozen roses were going to sway the likes of Barbara Blackwell, but that's not what mattered to me. What mattered was that starting the process of winning her back had finally begun. Doing so would take time, perseverance, ingenuity, and luck—but I was up for the challenge.

A challenge I'm determined to win.

I stood up from my desk and walked over to the wall of windows that overlooked Fifty-First Street. In the glass's reflection, I could see myself in the black Dior Homme business suit Barbara had purchased for me when we were together. On my wrist was the Hublot Classic Fusion watch she'd given to me for my birthday.

In my heart—always—was her.

Seeing her last night at Le Bernadin was just the beginning of a plan I'd been developing for years.

Now it was time for the next steps.

I turned away from the windows and considered my next move.

It's time to strategize, I thought. *And soon it will be time to go in harder. Just not yet . . .*

EIGHT
BARBARA

One week later

"I can't believe you're finally having me over to your new apartment."

I stood up from my desk and smiled at Jennifer, who was looking quite pretty in the belted wool blazer and matching pants she'd purchased last month at Bergdorf.

"Believe it," I said. "And by the way, Saint Laurent looks divoon on you but then it always does."

"Thank you."

"Actually, you should thank them—or at least convince your husband to buy them. The Gucci Group owns the brand now. With Wenn Fashion just getting started, imagine the flood of attention you'd receive from the media if it was announced that Laurent now belongs to Wenn. If you did that, everyone would take this new venture of yours seriously."

"They don't now?"

"We're talking fashion, darling, which is a world riddled with snobs, rage and regret, fragile egos, and impossibly high expectations. But you already know that because I've made sure to teach it to you over the years. Why start a new brand of your own when you can buy one that's already established and build upon that?" I arched my left eyebrow at her. "It's something to consider, you know?"

"I'm surprised you're not suggesting we buy Chanel."

"Who's to say that wasn't coming next?"

"Hilarious."

"Is it?" I asked as I walked around my desk and removed my coat from the closet. "You don't know it, darling, but I've been doing my research. If Wenn spent a few billion to purchase Laurent and Chanel, you could launch Wenn Fashion as a true luxury powerhouse. Look at LVHM, for instance. They own Tiffany, Bulgari, Fendi, Louis, Stella, Sephora, and Dior, for God's sake. And they make billions each year because of it."

I slipped into my coat and then reached for my clutch on the table next to me.

"But that's a conversation for another day. Have you secured a car for us with Cutter?"

"He's waiting for us now."

"Then let's go, because I need some advice."

"Since when do you need advice from me?"

"I've been in my apartment for only a few months, Jennifer, and I've yet to throw a dinner party there, let alone a Christmas Eve party. Since I need to get this right —and especially since you and Alex attend parties all the time and know what's on trend—I thought I should run my ideas by you first before I go all in, particularly because my apartment has its share of challenges."

"Barbara, you live at One57 on Billionaire's Row. What could possibly be the challenge?"

"You'll see," I said as I motioned toward the door. "Shall we?"

"OH WOW," Jennifer said after we left one of the apartment's three elevators and took a left, which revealed the massive great room and its dramatic views of the city and Central Park. "This is amazing—and we're so high up."

"Ninety floors."

"Unbelievable."

"We're also surrounded by floor-to-ceiling windows that I love but that also are causing an issue."

"What issue?"

"Why don't we walk around the room so that you can have a better sense of the space?"

"Take the lead."

For the next fifteen minutes, I motioned around the room, which was divided into three different areas with the help of strategically placed furniture. The off-white walls were in stark contrast to the dark-brown Brazilian wood floors gleaming beneath our feet.

Because this room was designed for entertaining, I'd decorated it with two enormous beige sofas that faced each other at the far right of the room. Each was firm, modern—and twenty feet long. Where the sofas ended were two Barcelona chairs in black leather, a single marble table between them, and then the windows—along with the views—at their backs.

"It's stunning," Jennifer said.

"You expected less?"

"Not at all."

We moved to the center of the room, where there was a smaller sitting area with an elegant curving sofa that could accommodate six comfortably, the two chairs that faced it, and a coffee table made of heavily lacquered wood. Each piece sat on a round custom-made rug, also off-white.

After we viewed the dining area, which was just off the kitchen at the room's far left and featured a hand-made crystal Lalique Cactus table that sat eight, I paused to look at Jennifer.

"Now that you've seen the space, where am I going to put the damned tree?"

"It's a Colorado blue spruce, you said?"

"That's right—and it's eleven feet tall. It's being delivered tomorrow, and I have no idea where it should go because this apartment is all about its views. Obstruct them with a giant tree—especially at night, with the city so beautiful and alive with lights—and I think you'll lessen the impact."

"How big is this room?"

I checked my nails.

"There you go again." I sighed. "Always the size queen."

"That would be Bernie," she said with a laugh. "Now answer my question."

"Fifty-seven by twenty-six."

She removed her SlimPhone from her jacket pocket, turned it on, opened the calculator app, and tapped a few numbers.

"This room is almost fifteen hundred square feet."

"Same at the master suite."

"Jesus—how big is the entire apartment?"

"Just over sixty-three hundred square feet. It has four bedrooms, five and a half baths, a chef's kitchen, an office, a media room, a library, loads of closet space, and so on. I've never told you this, but when I divorced Charles, my cut was thirty million dollars. When this came on the market, I knew I had to have it, so I bought it."

"Poor Charles."

"Said no one ever."

"Why so many bedrooms?"

"Why do you think?"

"In case Daniella and Alexa ever need to come back?"

"Precisely."

"I'm sorry you've been missing them."

"So am I, but let's not talk about that."

"Have you heard from Marcus?"

"Not a word, and it's been a blessing. But let's not discuss that either. We came here for a reason, Jennifer. Where do I put the tree?"

She looked across the room.

"If it were me, I'd get rid of the Barcelona chairs and put it over there," she said, pointing at them. "That way, when your guests arrive, the first thing they'll see when they leave the elevators is the tree."

"Oddly, I was contemplating the same thing."

"Think of it—you could hit them over the head with the tree and then with the views beyond it."

"I have to say the idea of somebody fainting from the sheer beauty of it all isn't just enticing; it's also flattering."

"Just up your liability insurance, OK?"

"Noted."

"I assume you're having Chanel decorate the tree?"

"Now you're just being cruel," I said. "If only they offered such a service."

"How about if I help you decorate it? We could make a day of it."

"I appreciate the offer, but the girls are coming over tomorrow evening for an early dinner and then we're going to decorate the tree together. Cutter also will be joining us because he's tall enough to handle the star."

"Assuming you don't poison them with your cooking."

"Cooking?" I said. "*I'm* not the one who will be doing the cooking, Jennifer."

"Who will?"

"The beauty of living here is that the Park Hyatt resides on the lower levels. Because of that, all residents have access to in-residence dining. When everyone is here, all I need to do is call the concierge, order dinner, and enjoy it when it arrives."

"Fancy," she said.

"It gets better," I said. "Say I wanted to have an impromptu cocktail party. All I need to do is call the concierge, tell him what I want, and they'll cater it at a moment's notice."

"Will you have them cater Christmas Eve?"

"To be determined," I said. "I'll need to try them out first."

"Imagine if they impress you."

"That's going to be a challenge, of course, but if they do, it will making living here almost effortless."

"So you'll put the tree over there?" she said.

"I think I will. Thank you for your help, Jennifer."

"My pleasure," she said. "Show me the rest of the place?"

"I'd love to give you a tour."

And that was true, because even though I'd never say it to Jennifer, just having someone else here was lifting my spirits.

When I bought this apartment, I thought starting over somewhere else would be the distraction I needed, particularly with the girls now living in apartments of their own. But after everything was settled and *this* apartment was fully furnished? I found myself fighting against moments of loneliness, something I knew I needed to resolve.

For years, my social life at home had revolved around Daniella and Alexa. But now? It was just me here, and although I never, ever thought I'd be weak enough to feel as if I'd become something as ridiculous as an empty nester—a phrase I detested to my core—apparently that's exactly what I was.

And I hated it.

It was an hour later, when the tour was over and

Jennifer had left to return home to Alex and Aiden, that I did something I had never done when I was alone—I made myself a martini, sat down on the edge of one of the sofas, and numbed myself a bit by sipping the drink while trying to adjust to my new normal.

Absolute silence.

NINE

BARBARA

Two days later—a Sunday—was a distracting whirlwind of activity, all of which I welcomed, if only so I could get out of my damned head.

At eight, I made coffee and glanced through the *Times*. At nine, I called Alexa to see if she'd be bringing anyone special with her tonight.

"There is no one special, Mom."

"I'm sorry," I said.

"It's fine. I mean, how many tree huggers live in this city?"

"I'd imagine you'd find plenty at Wenn Environmental."

"There are a few, but they have issues."

"What issues?"

"Wives and girlfriends."

"I see. Well, there *is* someone out there for you, my dear."

"Just as there is for you," she said. "His names is Marcus."

"Let's not go there."

"It's true—but I won't bother you with that."

"I appreciate it."

"At least not now anyway."

"Alexa . . ."

"Look, I was about to run some errands when you called. Can I bring anything tonight? Wine? Champagne?"

"I think we're good."

"Text me if you think of anything."

"I'll do that."

"Perfect. And at five, I'll look forward to seeing you and especially the fake tree I asked you to buy."

"Right," I said, deciding I'd deal with that disappointment when she arrived. If I told her now that the tree was real, she might not come at all—and I wanted her here. "See you at five."

"You'll be in full hair and makeup?"

That caused me to pause.

"That's an odd question. When aren't I?"

"Well, there's that."

"And why would you even ask? That's a question for your sister, who actually cares about that sort of thing."

"I'm asking because I plan to take a shitload of photos, and I know you'll be pissed if you don't look your best in them."

"That's never been an issue for me."

"How about giving me some points for being thoughtful?"

"That I can do. See you soon, love."

The tree was delivered an hour later, and it was as

tall and full as it was magnificent. After the delivery men placed it in the spot Jennifer and I had agreed upon in the great room, I tipped them before they left and then admired how the tree's silvery blue tones complemented the room's off-white walls and furniture. It gave the space a pop of color that would only intensify when it was strung with lights and decorated with my collection of antique ornaments.

Best of all, the room had so many windows, my concerns of impeding the view turned out to be unwarranted.

After tidying up the apartment, I chose a Christmas playlist on Spotify for when the girls and Cutter arrived, went to my office to finish up some work for Wenn, and then at four thirty—with the sun already set and the city fully alive with twinkling lights—I changed into my outfit for the evening before everyone arrived at five.

After the funk I fell into last night, I knew I had to wear something that would lift my mood. As such, I chose a pair of black slim-fitting satin pants with fabulous feather cuffs; a black micro-ribbed shirt with embellished buttons; and a pair of shiny, clear vinyl faux leather pumps, all by Fendi.

"They'll be expecting Chanel," I said to myself as I changed in front of my dressing room's oval mirror. "So why not surprise them with something else?"

At five sharp, the concierge called to tell me Alexa had arrived and was on her way up. I went to greet her, but when the elevator dinged and the stainless steel doors slid open, it wasn't Alexa who stepped out of the car and into the foyer.

Instead, it was Marcus.

With a fistful of red roses in his right hand.

Impeccably dressed in a black suit.

His thick silvery hair parted on the side, which made his ridiculously blue eyes appear even bluer.

For a moment, I just stared at him, stunned. For the first time in years, I didn't know what to say or do. That was unusual for me but so was this moment.

How did he get up here?

Before I could act or even process that I'd been set up by at least one of my daughters, with one bold move, he came toward me, tossed the roses on the table behind me, and took me in his arms, kissing me so gently on the lips, I somehow lost myself in the moment and found myself kissing him back.

It felt right.

But as the moment lingered, it also felt dangerous.

"Marcus, we can't," I said when our lips parted.

"And yet that kiss said we absolutely should."

Before I could respond, he took my face in his hands and kissed me again—but not only on my mouth. He also kissed the nape of my neck, an area that was so sensitive, I couldn't help but feel aroused.

And wanted.

Vulnerable.

Not so alone.

"Do me a favor," he said in my ear. "Don't overthink this."

"Do you even know me?"

He smiled at that, and I'd be lying to myself if I said I hadn't missed his smile.

"I've worked my ass off to have this moment," he said. "And here we are—at last." His eyes searched mine. "Where's your bedroom?"

"Marcus."

"I assume you have one, Barbara—where is it?"

"I have a tree to decorate."

"We can tend to that later."

"I have guests coming over."

"No, you don't. They've had a change of plans."

He turned his head to the side and kissed me again, but this time it was different. This time, his kiss was seared with passion. This time, he went all in. As he kissed me with a sense of urgency, he reached down, took my hands in his own, and then pressed his body against me so that I could feel his excitement throbbing against my thigh.

"If you want this to stop, just say so."

But I couldn't.

My emotions and my body were betraying me, and yet somehow I was caring less and less as he leaned in for another kiss. But that was the thing about Marcus—when it was just he and I in each other's presence, there was something about him that made me feel safe enough to drop the tough veneer I showed to the world.

Three years ago, I ended our relationship. During the past week, I found myself defending that position. But now? With him kissing me? My hands still in his? My heart beating so quickly as I drank in his masculine scent? I was beyond confused.

I'd been steadfast in my resolve not to allow him back into my life. But despite that, here he was nevertheless, his hands smoothing down my back and then curving around my ass in ways that were so seductive, it was almost too much to bear.

Will he hurt me again? I wondered as I placed my hand on his chest. *Do I ask him to leave? Or will I regret it if I do?*

I wasn't sure. But when Marcus suddenly lifted me off the floor and swept me into his arms, he asked me again where my bedroom was—and this time, after I glimpsed the determination on his face, I surprised myself by telling him it was just down the hallway behind him.

And that settled it.

As he carried me down the corridor, I lowered my head onto one of his broad shoulders and closed my eyes. We would make love again—and then? After my heart and body had been laid bare to him? It was in the wake of what happened next between us that I'd decide if I'd made the best or the worst decision of my life.

TEN
BARBARA

Two hours later, with the city's lights casting bright rainbow hues through my bedroom's floor-to-ceiling windows, Marcus and I were lying next to each other in my bed.

While my mind was whirling with questions about how we would move forward in the wake of such powerful intimacy, he was asleep and breathing soundly.

And why shouldn't he be? I thought.

After ninety minutes of lovemaking, which had been physically and emotionally intense for each of us, he was spent. And I couldn't blame him, especially since there was no part of my body that he hadn't tended to with meticulous intent.

Marcus was a fabulous, selfless lover. Like me, he had taken care of his body, which was lean, muscular, and ripped. I loved him in a suit, but I had to admit, I especially liked what he was wearing now—absolutely nothing.

But can I trust you? I thought as I looked at him. *Because if I can't, in the end, we have nothing.*

You need to get out of your head.

That's not going to happen.

Why are you treating him like Charles? Marcus didn't cheat on you—Charles did. In fact, Marcus only disappointed you. There's a huge difference here.

He still hurt me. He came into my life, I took a risk by falling for him, and then he hurt me. He could do it again.

Life is a risk, Barbara—

You think I don't know that?

What I know is that you're living it in fear. Worse, you're living in the rearview.

The rearview?

The past. Call it what you will, but you're living there. After all these years, you still can't shake what Charles did to you.

Bullshit.

It isn't bullshit. Are you really going to attach Charles's face to every man you meet? I thought you were stronger than that.

Everyone thinks I'm strong. It's their greatest misconception of me.

That's because all you show them is the facade.

I have my reasons.

And those reasons might cost you a good man. If you shut Marcus out a second time, you will lose him. Is that really what you want? To push away a man who's worked so hard to win you back because he's in love with you?

I don't trust easily.

Then I suggest you work on that. Because if you don't?

That silence that drove you to drink last night is going to be with you for the rest of your life. Is that also what you want? To be alone when you could be thriving with a man who would do anything for you?

Are you finished?

I am for now.

Then go.

Without waking Marcus, I stepped naked out of bed, slipped into the white Chanel robe I'd slung over a nearby armchair, and went into my master bath to freshen up.

When I looked at myself in the lighted mirror, the first thing I noticed was a glow I hadn't seen on my face for the past three years. Not even the use of expensive serums, toning mists, and luxurious creams could match what I was seeing now, and the reason wasn't lost on me.

The glow all came down to Marcus.

But countering it was the tension I saw in my eyes, a clear sign that grappling with my subconscious had gotten to me. And why not? She'd given me a lecture, and there were a lot of things said that I couldn't deny.

Against my better judgment, I'd made love to Marcus, and it had been fantastic. The magic was still there. But would it always be? That was a ridiculous question no one could answer.

But I did know this. I needed to decide soon whether it would be worth the risk to find out.

ELEVEN
MARCUS

When I woke, I checked my watch, noted it was nearly eight, and then reached out my hand for Barbara—who wasn't lying next to me. I turned my head, saw that she wasn't there, and was about to call out to her when the hum of the master bath's fan stopped me.

A moment later, when she started to run the shower, I knew that was my cue to act.

We might have made love once, I thought. *But why not twice?*

I slid naked out of bed and stepped into the spacious bathroom, at the far right of which was a large glass-enclosed shower that easily could accommodate eight, never mind two. Barbara's beautiful, slender back was facing me as she used her fingers to test the water for the right temperature.

Had she even heard me enter the bathroom?

Doubtful, because if she had, I'd know it. I didn't want to frighten her, so I knocked on the door behind me and waited for her reaction.

When she looked over her shoulder at me, at first she searched my eyes before she said, "There's room for two in here, Marcus." She glanced down at my heavy erection, which was throbbing in front of me. "But I fear there might be no room for that."

And that was all the invitation I needed.

When I stepped into the shower, I already knew the drill—don't get her hair wet or "Bernie will have my ass." So I didn't. Instead, I reached for a plush white towel from a rack inside the shower, tossed it at her feet on the tile floor, and kneeled in front of her, pressing my mouth against her sex as I did so.

The first night we made love three years ago, she said when we finished that she'd never had oral sex before, which told me everything I needed to know about Charles. It was after that admittance that I realized, during the first year we spent together, that I had to show Barbara things her first husband likely had never taught her.

Within reason. Barbara was, after all, first and foremost a lady. But she also had a curious mind that was eager to try new things.

In the end, she became a quiet yet passionate lover—with one exception. Despite how gentle I was, she couldn't help the low moan that escaped her lips when I entered her, especially when I reached around and cupped her breasts in my hands, lightly tweaking her nipples as I did so.

Like I was now.

Later, when our lovemaking was over, we each washed the other with unscented soap. I didn't want to smell like a flower—and I was happy I didn't have to. As Barbara washed my chest, I told her so.

"Of course it's unscented," she said. "I mean, why would any woman be stupid enough to wear two competing scents?"

"Two competing scents?"

"You're such a man," she said with a smile. "Let me be clear. Imagine if I used Coco Mademoiselle Gel Moussant and then molested it with another brand crafted by another designer? I'd smell like a goddamn whore."

"You know, I think my ex-wife used to do that."

She slapped me on my ass. "You've come a long way, darling."

"You don't have to tell me that twice."

"Shall we get dressed and trim the tree?"

"Trim the tree?"

"Yes, trim the tree. You may have hijacked this evening to have your way with me—twice, I might add—but there is still a tree that needs to be trimmed. And you're just tall enough to tend to the star."

"I thought I just did."

For a moment, she seemed to assess me with new eyes before she slipped into her plush white robe and swept by me. "Very clever. Why don't you get dressed? I'll meet you in the living room."

"You want me to trim the tree in a business suit?"

"Or your birthday suit—either would be fine with me."

"Your entire apartment is comprised of windows. The whole city would see me."

"Perhaps they should."

"You must have something I can wear."

She moved to speak but then paused when she glanced at the adjoining dressing room.

"Do you?" I asked.

"It's not what you think," she said.

"What am I thinking?"

"Oh, I don't know, Marcus—probably that I have a trail of men coming through here nightly."

"Nah," I said. "That isn't you."

"And you'd be right." She put her hand on her hips and sighed. "When we were together, you kept a pair of sweatpants and a couple of T-shirts in my old apartment for those evenings you slept over. When I moved here, I came upon them."

"And you didn't throw them out?"

"Let's not psychoanalyze the situation."

"But why would you keep them?"

She stepped into the dressing room and returned a moment later with a pair of black sweats and a white T-shirt. She handed them to me.

"Just be happy I did," she said. "Now change. In the meantime, I'll go to the living room, call the concierge, and ask him to bring us something to nibble on since neither of us have had dinner. You must be famished."

"I could eat."

"Martini?"

"That also could work."

"Everything will be here quicker than you think," she said as she turned to leave. "They're efficient. So don't be too long, OK?"

"I won't."

When she was gone, I stood there rethinking my day. Earlier that morning, when I reached out to Alexa to see if she could manage a meeting between her mother and me, she said she could do better than a mere meeting. And so, with her sister's and Cutter's help, all of them set the table for this to happen, which included Alexa meeting me in the lobby so that she could assure security that I could take the elevator alone.

I was beyond grateful to all of them, especially because everything went far better than I ever could have imagined.

Barbara and I made love, we showered and made love again, and now she just revealed that she's held on to these clothes for the last three years. Why? Why would she do that? She could have chosen to toss them out during the move, but she didn't. Does that mean she still feels the love I have for her? Are these clothes proof that she wanted to keep some part of me with her?

Whatever the case, I had a tree to trim, food and drink to share with the love of my life, and a surprise to spring on her when the moment was right.

Will she agree to go with me? I wondered as I slipped into the sweatpants and pulled the T-shirt over my head. *That's the question, because when it comes to Barbara? Who is unpredictable to her core?*

I shook my head.

I don't know whether she will or not . . .

TWELVE

BARBARA

So who are we now? I wondered as I walked down the hallway and moved into the living room. *Is it that easy? Just have sex and suddenly you're a couple again?*

You said you were going to take the risk, so maybe it is that easy. Do you regret making love with him?

No.

Did you feel safe? Loved?

More than I have in years.

Then you have your answer. Now I suggest you enjoy what life has given you.

And what's that?

A second chance. Not many get one, but you did. And that's all because of Marcus, who has gone out of his way to convince you to take him back. Are you just going to ignore that? I wouldn't. Take the risk.

"I have two amazing views competing for my attention," Marcus said behind me as he entered the room. "There's the city, and there's you. But which one wins?"

He crossed over to me, wrapped his arms around my waist, kissed me softly on my neck, and smoothed his hands down the length of my body before he pressed his lips against my right ear. "You win," he whispered. "But you'll always win with me."

At that moment, with his strong arms holding me tight, I closed my eyes and made my decision. I'd take the risk. I'd open my heart to him again. But if I was going to do so, it would have to be with baby steps.

Take the leap . . .

I turned to face him.

"I have a confession to make," I said.

He furrowed his brow. "A confession?"

"And I'm afraid you're not going to like it."

"OK"

"And now I'm wondering if I should even tell you at all."

"Barbara, you can tell me anything."

"Are you sure about that?"

"I am. Tell me."

"It's bleak," I said.

"Bleak?"

"I haven't called the concierge."

He blinked. "That's your confession?"

"You were expecting food and a martini, and yet I have neither."

I could see him trying to suppress a smile and was delighted when he couldn't do so.

"So what you're really saying is that you've been naughty."

"Yes, but unintentionally so," I said, motioning toward the windows surrounding us. "It's the view. It always stops me, particularly at night." I reached for his hand and held it tightly. "I become entranced by the glimmering lights."

"Paralyzed by them?"

"Exactly."

"Then how about if *I* call the concierge and get things rolling?"

"Would you?"

"Where's the phone?"

I motioned toward the sitting area in the center of the room. "It's over there on the side table," I said. "Just press the button marked 'concierge.'"

"What would you like?"

"A martini, of course. As for food, when I was in the process of moving, the girls and I ordered the New York cheese plate and the vegetable crudité, which are very good."

He kissed me on the forehead. "Then we'll have them."

"And then we'll trim the tree?" I asked.

"Then we'll trim the tree."

After he ordered, he hung up the phone and started to walk back to me. Watching him, I thought if there ever was a man who should wear tight sweats and an even tighter T-shirt, it was Marcus. His years of skiing had done his body well.

"Before we start with the tree, I have a question," he said.

"What's that?"

"Now that word's out that I'm back in the city, I've been invited to several Christmas parties, but only one interests me."

"Mine?"

"That goes without saying—if you'll have me, naturally I'll be here."

"Consider yourself invited."

When he smiled at me, I could tell he was pleased.

"Which party were you talking about?" I asked.

"Bill and Maxine Witherhouse's."

"Maxine Witherhouse? But that woman is an impossible snob."

"I know she is, which is why I try to deal mostly with Bill, who is easier to work with. Anyway, they've asked me to attend their annual Christmas party at their mansion on Fifth. Even though they're clients of mine, my interest in going has less to do with them and more to do with seeing their property. It was built in 1899 in the French Renaissance style for Ian Fletcher, a successful banker and railroad investor. You know how much I enjoy studying architecture. And their home is one of the last remaining mansions in the city. I'd like to see it." He reached for my hand. "And I'd like to see it with you at my side. Will you go with me?"

"When is it?"

"In three days. I know that's short notice, but I hope you'll still consider it."

"Three days starting today?" I asked. "Or three days starting tomorrow?"

"Good point," he said. "Starting today."

"And yet today is nearly over, so really I'd have only two days to prepare for Maxine's little shindig."

"Think of it as a challenge."

Pulling together a look in two days would be a challenge, but with the help of Bernie, Bergdorf, and maybe a dash of Balenciaga, I knew I could do it. What concerned me was something more personal.

"If you and I show up together in that crowd, you know we'll cause a stir," I said. "Are you prepared for that?"

"I'd welcome it."

"They'll think we're a couple again."

"Are we? Because I want to be. I'm in love with you, Barbara. I've never stopped loving you. But I get it. I know you never expected me to enter your life again. And because of that, I also know you probably need time to sit with your feelings. My only hope is that one day you'll also say you're in love with me."

This was all unfolding so quickly, my head was spinning.

Am I still in love with him? I wondered. I wasn't sure, but since Marcus was nothing short of a gentleman, he didn't push.

"Look," he said after a moment. "As for being a couple, if you're not ready to commit to that now, all we need to say to anyone who inquires about the status of our relationship is that we've decided to start seeing each other again."

And that was all it took—witnessing his kindness again. His compassion. They were among his best traits.

He is in love with me, I thought. *There's no questioning it.*

And so I made my decision. I placed the palm of my hand over his heart and looked him in the eyes.

"I'll go to the party with you," I said.

His face lit up.

"You will?"

"I will."

"As my date? Or—"

"As your date," I said. "Baby steps, OK?"

"I can do baby steps."

And that was all I needed to ease back into myself.

"Perfect," I said. "But just so you know, those baby steps also include intimacy."

"I'm glad to hear it."

"Well, I'm not a complete idiot, Marcus. You're a fabulous lover. After today, of course I want more." Before he could speak, I lowered my voice to a whisper. "And better yet, since we're officially dating again, no one can call me a whore."

"If they did, they'd have to deal with me."

"How completely alpha of you."

"Do you want to go back to the bedroom and see how alpha I can be?"

"But you've already shown me twice today."

"That was nothing."

"How intriguing."

From the foyer, the elevator dinged.

"I think our food and drinks just arrived," I said.

"Of course they have."

"Would you mind?" I asked. "I'd hate to greet them in my robe."

"I'll take care of it," he said.

It was later, after we enjoyed our martinis and the food, and then trimmed the tree, that he led me to my bedroom and took care of me again and again.

THIRTEEN
BARBARA

The next morning, I woke with Marcus at my side. We made love for the fourth time in two days, and after showering with him, I got my ass in gear, fixed my hair, applied my makeup, and chose the stunning black Chanel suit I'd purchased the week before.

"What's the hurry?" Marcus asked as I slipped into a pair of black Valentino pumps. "It's like you're on speed."

I looked across the room at him. Typical for a man, he was already showered, shaved, dressed, and ready to take on the world.

"I need to get to work early," I said. "And for good reason. I have two days to find something perfect to wear to Maxine's party. Jennifer doesn't know it yet, but I'm hijacking her today for a trip to Bergdorf. I want her opinion on which gown I should choose. You'll be in black tie?"

"I will. And after the party, when I take you home, I'll change into my birthday suit so that I can take you to another planet."

"You're insatiable."

"You make me insatiable. Like I told you, I haven't been with another woman since you."

He had mentioned that to me before, and it still surprised me. Whenever I'd thought of him over the years, I'd simply assumed that because of his good looks and success, he must have found somebody else.

I was so wrong about him, I thought with a stab of guilt. *And I've yet to apologize for how I handled things.*

Before I left for Wenn, I stood in front of a long oval mirror, checked my look, and saw Marcus watching me in the reflection. When our eyes met, I turned to him.

"I need to say something to you," I said.

"OK."

"I wish I'd handled things differently when I ended our relationship. I never should have broken up with you over the phone—and so casually. As if you didn't matter to me. You did, of course. More than you know. But I was acting out of hurt." I shook my head. "I've been hurt more times in my life than anyone knows. It's why I act the way I do—never show any signs of weakness. Always have the thickest skin in the room. Distract with humor and bitchy asides. That's who I am."

"And that's the person I love."

"That might be, but what I should have done was tell you how frustrated I was becoming with our relationship, but my pride wouldn't allow it. My pride told me that you should have *instinctively* known I was missing you and that it was on you to fix it."

I rolled my eyes at myself.

"I was a fool, Marcus. I should have given you the

benefit of the doubt, and I didn't. I should have told you how I was feeling, but I didn't do that, either. I want to apologize to you for that."

He smiled.

"I appreciate that, Barbara."

"It's the least I can do given the way I behaved. We lost three years because of me."

"You had a right to your feelings."

"True, but I didn't have the right to blow things up between us in the process."

"Do you think we'd still be together today if you had told me how you were feeling?"

"I'd like to think so."

"I know we'd still be together, but let's not focus on the past. Let's focus on the present. When can I see you again?"

"The night of the party? I'd like to say sooner, but I need to find a gown. I need Bernie to color my hair. There's work to be done at Wenn. And I need to get some emergency Botox—as in today."

"You don't need Botox."

"You say that because you haven't known me without it."

"You could be flooded with wrinkles and I wouldn't care."

"But I would, so I need to make that appointment."

"All right," he said. "How about if we have a drink here before going to the Witherhouse's? We can spend some time alone before the event and also enjoy a cocktail."

"But that would mean consuming calories," I said.

"Sorry?"

"I wasn't thinking of eating or drinking anything until *after* the party."

His eyes widened when I said that.

"Clearly it's time for an intervention," he said. "You need to eat and drink something, Barbara."

"I also have to keep my figure."

"You have the body of a thirty-year-old."

"And here I was shooting for twenty-five."

"Come on," he said. "We'll have a drink and go to the party and then just think of the calories you'll burn when I take you home and get you into bed. After I'm finished with you, it'll be like you never ate or drank anything at all."

"How oddly convincing," I said.

"So you'll have that drink with me?"

"I mean, when you put it that way, why wouldn't I?"

"Perfect. How does seven sound?"

"Seven sounds fine."

"I want to spend as much time with you as I can, Barbara."

"And we're going to work on that. Just remember that I never saw this coming, and I still have things on my calendar that I've previously committed to."

"Trust me when I say there's no pressure."

"I appreciate that. And who knows? Perhaps when I return to the office and have a look at my schedule, I can loosen things up a bit."

"That would be great."

I checked the time on my watch. "I need to leave," I said. "Bergdorf may open at eleven, but to secure Jennifer for an entire afternoon, I need to ask before her workday begins."

"Understood. Share a taxi? I need to go back to my apartment and change into a fresh suit before I head to the office."

"Of course."

I reached for his hand, and we started for the foyer's bank of elevators.

"Thanks for listening to me," I said.

He squeezed my hand.

"Anytime. And Barbara?"

"What's that?"

"Thanks for agreeing to take those baby steps."

FOURTEEN
BARBARA

"So let me see if I understand you correctly," I said to Jennifer as she took the chair opposite my desk at Wenn. It was just past seven, and just as they always were, she and Alex were already at work. "You and Alex are also going to Maxine's party?"

"We just decided last night, Barbara."

"Does she know yet?"

"I called her to accept this morning."

"Do you know who else is going?"

"I imagine Maxine will invite many people we know. But when it comes to our closest friends, I know Epifania and Rudman will be there. Kate and Ben will be there."

"Lisa and Tank?"

"Unfortunately, no."

"The sheer rudeness of it all."

"I don't think they even know Maxine and Bill."

"Lucky them," I said. Then I decided it was time to discuss what neither of us wanted to talk about. *But I still have to mention it.* "I'm sure you know this will be the first time Maxine has entertained at her home since the shooting."

"I do know that," she said. "It's been four years since that night, so at least she respected the dead and waited before throwing another party. But I'm not going to lie to you—going back there is going to give me some serious PTSD, Barbara. I saw Diana Crane and Mike Fine die that night. I saw them get shot in the street. And I saw too many others lose their lives as well."

"And all because of that madman, Stephen Rowe."

"Thank God he's dead."

"If attending the party will upset you, why go?"

"To prove that I can move beyond that day. We might never mention that night because it's too painful to relive it, but it still haunts me. I still see a therapist because of it. I could have lost Alex that night. He could have lost me. It's unshakable what Rowe did to all of us—especially to those who lost their lives."

"This won't be easy."

"It won't, but I have to do it. If I don't, Rowe will have won again."

"Then I commend you. You're being very brave, my dear. How does Alex feel?"

"The same—he wants to face his own demons."

"I'm happy I'll be there to face them with each of you."

"I am too. But enough of that," I said. "Let's change the mood with a new subject."

"And what's that?"

"Alexa told me Marcus dropped by to see you yesterday. How did that go?"

"We'll discuss that at another time."

"Why? Maxine mentioned you're going to the party with him, so I have to assume you two talked and at least worked a few things out."

"We did, but I don't want to get ahead of it. Let's just say I'm still absorbing everything that happened."

"Tell me when you're ready?"

"I will. Now about the party. We need to go to Bergdorf and find something to wear."

"I have plenty to wear."

"Darling, you have nothing to wear."

"Are you serious? I should be ashamed of how many clothes I own."

"Looking good when you and Alex are busy striking deals at the events you attend is critical to Wenn's success. And I'll be damned if anyone sees you in the same outfit twice."

"Fine. What time would you like to go?"

"Noon. I'll call Cutter and ask him to drive us."

"What are you hoping to find?"

"Oh, I don't know, Jennifer. Maybe something fabulous? Something *dramatic*?"

"Something sexy for Marcus?"

"One never knows."

"Whatever it is, you'll find it there."

"And you?"

She shrugged. "Everyone is going to be at that party, including the press. So probably a gown?"

"That's what I was thinking for you, but it needs to be next level. I've already sent Bernie a text to see if he can color my hair tomorrow morning. How about if I text him again to see if he can do our makeup before the party?"

"I'd love that."

"You just want to hear his racy stories."

"Can you blame me?"

"Actually, I can't," I said. "And by the way, we'll have to meet with him in the midafternoon. At seven, Marcus is coming over to my apartment for a drink before we leave for the party."

"I'm living for all of this," she said as she checked the time on her watch. "I'm going to be late for my first meeting. Are we good here?"

"We're good."

As she stood from her seat and turned to leave, I admired her for a moment. She was wearing her long dark-brown hair down today, which looked especially beautiful, likely because Bernie had colored and styled it just last week.

"See you at noon," she said.

"I'll call Chloe at ten thirty, book a private appointment with her, and also give her an idea of what we're seeking."

"Considering how you've treated her over the years, let's hope she even takes your call."

"I'm not *that* harsh with her. I simply expect perfection."

"As if perfection exists."

I eased back in my chair.

"It does in my world, darling. Now shoo. There's work to do. I'll see you at noon."

LATER, when Jennifer and I met Cutter in the garage so that he could take us to Bergdorf, I asked her if Tank's parents were still planning to come for Christmas.

"Oh, it's on," Jennifer said after we were seated in the limousine. "Ethel is determined to come. Worse, she's also determined to stay at their home."

"How awful."

"I know."

"Here's an idea—if Lisa fills their bedroom with a slew of her zombie novels, there's a good chance Ethel might combust."

"From your mouth to Satan's ears."

Cutter stepped behind the wheel, started the car, and then we were off to Bergdorf.

"When are they arriving?" I asked.

"Who knows? Ethel keeps changing the dates."

"Which is making it challenging for Lisa to make plans."

"Exactly."

"She truly is a risible person."

"And to think someone as good as Tank came out of her womb."

"Poor Tank—they probably had to use the Jaws of Life just to free him from her."

"There's an image."

"Here's another—I bet her vagina has teeth."

"Oh man," Cutter said.

"It's true, Cutter," I said. "And you and I both know they're razor sharp."

"Anyway," Jennifer said. "To your point about Lisa distracting them as much as possible while they're here, she took your advice."

"Do tell."

"They'll be dining out every night, they'll shop and do some sightseeing during the day, and when they can, they'll catch a few shows."

"Even if Ethel does keep changing her dates, all of that is doable, but do you think it will be enough?"

"It's their first time in the city," she said. "I certainly hope so."

"I wouldn't count on it. And just so you know, if Ethel misbehaves at *my* party? I'm not above slipping her a roofie, waiting ten minutes for it to kick in, and then filming her unhinged antics with my SlimPhone. As one of my Christmas gifts to Lisa, I'll send her the footage, and she can threaten to post it on Facebook should Ethel get out of line."

Jennifer smiled.

"What would we do without you?" she asked.

"Suffer fools?"

Ten minutes later, we arrived at Bergdorf. Chloe met us at the entrance and asked if either of us would like a glass of champagne after she took us to one of the private dressing rooms on the third floor.

"Well, I don't know, Chloe," I said as Jennifer and I sat down on a chic black sofa. "The last time I was here, the champagne was burned."

"I can assure you it won't be this time, Ms. Blackwell."

"But can you assure me it won't be flat? Because as you well know, it has been in the past."

"No, it hasn't," Jennifer said.

"Yes, it has."

"Every time you've said that, I've seen bubbles in your glass."

"And here I've always viewed them as a series of last gasps."

"God, you're impossible."

"Of course I'm impossible. If I wasn't, I wouldn't be here." I looked at Chloe and deepened my voice. "We'll try the champagne," I said to her. "And then you can bring in the gowns. We'll begin with what you have in mind for Jennifer."

"Absolutely, Ms. Blackwell," Chloe said and then she opened the door to her right and disappeared from sight.

"Why is she calling you by your last name?" Jennifer whispered. "She always calls you Barbara."

"I couldn't give a damn."

"I think it's out of fear."

"You would. I, on the other hand, think it's out of respect. We've spent a fortune here over the years—and our dear Chloe has benefited from every bit of it. I can't imagine how much money she's made off us, but I know it's been plenty."

"She's just doing her job."

"And I'm only toying with her. Chloe knows it. You know it. The universe knows it. So, please, let me have my fun."

I expected her to clap back, but instead, she seemed to study me for a moment.

"There's something different about you," she said.

"Pray tell, what?"

"You're back to being yourself. Last week, you were having none of it because you wanted nothing to do with Marcus. But now?" She narrowed her eyes. "Now there's a glow about you. And I think I know why. You've already slept with him."

"So now I'm a whore?"

"No. I'm just calling you out. You've slept with him. I know it."

"You know nothing."

"Your legs might be crossed now, but they weren't yesterday."

At that moment, Chloe returned to the room carrying a silver tray with two flutes of bubbling champagne. She offered a glass to each of us.

"It's delicious, Chloe," Jennifer said after her first sip. "Thank you."

"It's my pleasure, Jennifer."

When Chloe turned to me, she looked surprised when I handed her my empty glass. With Jennifer needling so relentlessly around my personal life, which I didn't want to discuss—at least not yet—I'd downed the champagne.

"That was actually quite good, Chloe," I said to her. "Bring me another? Then we'll get on with choosing a gown that suits."

"I'll be back in a moment."

"A fraction of a moment, if you can."

Jennifer raised an eyebrow.

"So you don't want to be left alone with me now that I'm on to you?" she asked when Chloe left.

She's like a dog with a bone, and she's not letting go of this anytime soon. Just tell her and be done with it.

"Fine," I said. "We had sex."

"I knew it!"

"It's that obvious?"

"Only to those who know you well, so don't worry about it." She leaned toward me and said in a low voice, "How was it?"

"I'm certainly not answering that here," I said. "We have reputations to uphold, for God's sake."

"Fine," she said. "Just one last question. Are you back together?"

"We've agreed to take things slowly." When her eyes widened, I held up my right index finger. "Lose the moon eyes, darling. We are *not* a couple. We are simply dating."

"When will you see him again?"

"Before he left my apartment this morning, he asked if we could have a drink before the party."

"So he spent the night?"

I rolled my eyes and didn't answer.

"This is so exciting, I can't stand it."

When Chloe entered the room with a glass of champagne for me and a rack of gowns for us to assess, I gave Jennifer a look so stern, it wiped the giddiness off her face.

"And what do you have here, Chloe?" I asked as she handed me a second glass of champagne. I stood from the sofa and glanced over the sea of gowns. "I see Ralph, De La Renta, Jason Wu, Balenciaga, McQueen, Tom Ford,

Akris, Versace, Saint Laurent, Carolina Herrera, and even Naeem Khan. Well done."

"Thank you, Ms. Blackwell."

"I assume that new tailor of yours, Simon, is here today?"

"He is."

"And he's prepared to tend to us before we leave?"

"I told him myself to drop everything the moment you and Jennifer have made your decisions."

"Perfect."

I turned to Jennifer.

"Choose," I said. "After you do, Chloe will show me the gowns she's selected for me, we'll try them on, we'll assess, and if we have chosen well, Simon can get to work."

Four hours later, we left Bergdorf with two stunning gowns, each tailored to fit by Simon. With my approval, Jennifer chose a velvet petal strapless trumpet gown by Marchesa while I went with the Missandra gown by Ralph Lauren. With its column silhouette, allover sequin embellishment, boat neckline, long sleeves, open back, and floor-sweeping design, the gown was a showstopper.

"I think we did well," Jennifer said.

"I agree. Would you mind if Cutter drops me at my apartment? I don't want to risk anything happening to this gown."

"Not at all. Cutter, would you take Barbara home, please?"

"Of course," he said.

"Before we drop you off, I wanted to ask if you needed any help with the Christmas Eve party," she said.

"I have everything covered."

"There's a surprise. Do tell."

While Cutter drove, we discussed the party, which was less than two weeks away. Now that the tree was up and the invitations were out, the pressure was essentially off, especially since I'd decided to have the Park Hyatt cater the event. They had a five-star chef, the menu they'd presented to me was fab, and I'd secured two servers through them as well as a bartender. Three days before the party, a friend of mine—a retired Broadway designer with five Tonys to his credit—would see to the decorating.

"Oh, just the five Tonys?" Jennifer said when I told her. "Such a letdown."

"Very funny. The designs he emailed me were divoon."

"I'd expect nothing less from you. Soon we'll need to go shopping for your party as well."

"How about next week?"

"Let's."

"Will Marcus be there on Christmas Eve?"

"He will."

"That makes me happy," she said. "I can't wait to talk with him again. But about Maxine's party. You do realize when you show up at Maxine's with Marcus on your arm, people are going to lose their minds?"

"Not if we arrive with you and Alex. If we do, all the attention will be on both of you."

"But only for a moment."

"True, but that moment will nevertheless allow me to get inside before they have a chance to question us."

"Good point—we'll go as a team. Alex likes Marcus."

"The feeling is mutual."

Cutter pulled alongside my building.

"Let me help you with your things, Barbara," he said as he stepped out of the car and opened my door.

"No need, darling boy," I said as I joined him on the sidewalk with my clutch in one hand and the bag from Bergdorf in the other. "You're in a relationship with my daughter, which has to be exhausting. I suggest you reserve your strength for her."

"I'm happy to help," he said.

"Marry her and one day I'll let you."

"That day is coming, Barbara."

"And here I thought it would never happen."

"It will happen."

"Good, because you've dated her long enough, and it's time for you to become my son-in-law."

"I can't wait for that day," he said.

"Neither can I, Cutter," I said, meaning it. "You'll make a terrific addition to our family."

"Thanks for your help with the gown," Jennifer said from the car.

"My pleasure," I said. "And thank you for keeping your mouth shut about everything we discussed earlier."

"My lips are sealed."

"They better be."

And then I was gone.

FIFTEEN

MARCUS

Two days later
Hours before the Witherhouse party

Could time go any slower? I wondered in frustration. *It's been two days since I last saw her. We've talked on the phone each night, and we've sent plenty of texts, but that's just a tease. And I have three more meetings to attend before I can bust out of here so that we can have that drink before the party.*

For the past five hours, I'd been stuck at my office at Koch Capital Advisors.

Before the markets opened, I'd done what I do every business day. I'd reviewed our fund's current position by looking at yesterday's reports from Jonathan, my best friend and portfolio manager. I'd met with my staff to discuss new trading opportunities. I'd pored over financial news, caught up on emails and phone calls, monitored the markets when they opened, adjusted trades, and considered new opportunities as they arose.

And that was just a slice of it.

I loved my job, but with Barbara back in my life, it was a struggle to stay focused on it, something Jon noted when we had lunch in my office two hours ago. My executive assistant, Harlow, had ordered takeout for us at the Capital Grille. Since Jon was a fitness freak like me, we each had the Maine lobster salad with a citrus vinaigrette and called it good.

In the fifteen minutes I had before my next meeting, I thought back to our lunch and recalled what had been said.

Because Jon's insights were that important.

"WHAT'S ON YOUR MIND, BUDDY?" *Jon asked as I picked at my salad. "You seem tense."*

We were sitting opposite each other at the conference table overlooking Fifty-First Street. At fifty-nine, we were the same age and shared similar interests, but there was one major difference between us—unlike me, Jon had never been divorced. Instead, he had Ellen, his amazing wife of thirty-one years. They were a successful, smart, great-looking couple whose love for each other was something to be admired.

It was, in fact, everything I wanted to have with Barbara.

Jon and I had been best friends for so long, he was the only person in my life I could trust implicitly. That's why he already knew I'd gone to see Barbara the other day, that we'd made love while I was there, and that we'd agreed to start seeing each other again.

I looked at him.

"Concerned is a better word," I said.

"Why the concern?"

"I don't know," I said in an effort to wave it off. "It's probably nothing. I think I'm just in my head."

"There has to be a reason, Marcus."

Just tell him.

"It's Barbara," I said. "The longer I'm away from her, the more I think something will go wrong between us."

"Why? Things are going well between you right now."

"That's the key," I said. "Right now they are. But how long will that last? Because Barbara is nothing if not unpredictable. And I know for a fact that regaining her trust will be an ongoing challenge."

"Go on."

"You know the story."

"Her first husband cheated on her and then you went on the missing person list."

"Right. My concern is that old wounds don't heal. As great as the other night was, a part of me feels that at any point, she's going to get cold feet and drop me again because she's determined not to get hurt. When I stepped out of her elevator the other day, I somehow convinced her to let her guard down, but how long will that last? It's the not knowing that's driving me crazy."

"Do you want my two cents?"

"I do."

"Two things. First, you need to get out of your damned head and live in the moment."

"I know I do," I said. "This isn't like me."

"It isn't, but I get it. You're in love with her, and you'll do anything to get her back. But here's the thing—women always know when something is off. They always know when someone—especially their man—is distracted. You don't want that because distraction can open the door for interpretation. And if that interpretation is negative?" He shook his head. "Trust me, you don't want that. Just be yourself and treat her like a queen."

"That's my plan," I said. "What else?"

"Now that she's willing to date you again, you need to be patient with her. Really patient. And then one day, if you do everything right, she will come to trust you again. But in the meantime, you're going to have to tread really fucking lightly."

"Thanks, Jon."

"No problem. And don't forget this—she's agreed to attend the Witherhouse's Christmas party with you, which means she's willing to go public with your relationship. That's a win for you, Marcus. That alone tells me she's serious about giving this another go."

"I can't mess it up, Jon."

"You won't. Just be your charming self—that's enough."

"You forgot handsome," I said with a smile.

He stabbed a piece of lobster with his fork and pointed it at me with a sad shake of his head. "Actually, I didn't."

WE'D LAUGHED AT THAT, which turned out to be just what I needed. Jon was right. I had to get out of my head.

She dismissed me at Le Bernadin, but she didn't when I showed up a week later at her apartment. Maybe she just needed time to process everything. I had to remember that.

I checked my watch, saw it was nearly time for my meeting, and stood up from my desk. I was excited for tonight and was looking forward to seeing the Witherhouse's mansion, but I was especially hoping the night would end with me in Barbara's bed.

"We'll see," I said to myself as I gathered the papers I needed for the meeting. "After all, she's the one who said the baby steps we're taking should also include intimacy . . ."

SIXTEEN

BARBARA

"These," Daniella said to me. We were in my walk-in closet sifting through rows upon rows of designer shoes. I'd asked her to drop by my apartment after work to help me choose the best footwear for my gown. "Classic Louboutins," she said. "Black, chic, sexy, and elegant." She looked at me and winked. "In other words, everything you need to get laid."

I leveled her with a glance before I admired the shoes when she dangled them in front of me. They were not only gorgeous but also a perfect complement to my gown. If I added a smattering of diamonds at my ears, wrists, and neck, it could be the knockout look I was hoping for.

"They are beautiful," I said.

"I love them. I mean, when you pair these with that gown, you essentially are going to become your own red-light district."

"Well, now I'm not wearing them at all."

"Don't be silly," she said as she brought them to me.

"Here. You'll thank me later." She tilted her head to one side and looked at me. "You saw Bernie today?"

"Jennifer and I both did."

"He knocked your hair and makeup out of the park."

"You should see what he did with Jennifer."

"Jennifer always looks good."

"Bernie's magic made her look fantastic."

She looked seriously at me.

"Have fun with Marcus tonight, OK?"

"I plan to."

When I took the shoes from her, I remembered Cutter's words from only a few hours ago—he said it wouldn't be long before he married Daniella. A part of me wanted to share that information with my daughter, but there was no way I was going to ruin Cutter's moment when he finally got down on one knee and proposed to her.

But it's coming, I thought. *One day soon they'll be married, and before long, I'll have my first grandchild to spoil.*

They had been dating and living together for years. It was time for them to fully commit to each other. It was time for marriage, and when that moment came? I planned to use my own money to throw them a wedding that was so spectacular, they'd never forget it.

To hell with Charles, I thought. *Let him spend his money on his slut of a wife, Rita.*

"Are we good?" she asked. "Cutter and I are having a date night tonight, and I need to run home so I can get ready."

"You're having a date night?"

"We are. He's taking me to dinner."

"At that Irish pub you two like so much?"

"No. Get this—he's taking me to Per Se."

"Per Se? Very nice."

"Right? He couldn't care less about expensive restaurants, but he knows I sometimes need my next-level fix, so he's taking me there."

"Enjoy yourself, my dear."

"And you have fun with Marcus at the party," she said. "Now give me a kiss, because I need to go."

I gave her a kiss on each cheek.

"You really like him, don't you?" I asked.

"Marcus? I love him. He checks all the boxes for me."

"All of them?"

"Every one. I'm so glad you agreed to give him another chance. I know Alexa feels the same. He's so not Dad."

"Oddly, I couldn't agree more."

"You deserve someone like him, Mom."

"Your approval of him means a lot to me, you know?"

"I'm glad it does. Look, he made one mistake, and he went out of his way to fix it. That says everything to me about his character and also about how much you mean to him. He never stopped loving you, Mom. And what's happening now? With him back in your life? It's like you're a character in your own romance novel. In fact, consider this your very own second-chance romance."

"You must stop reading those awful romance books."

"Never—they give me life."

"Please."

"Have you read Christina Ross? One of her characters reminds me of you."

"I'll sue!"

"Now I really have to go," she said as she left the closet. "I'll call you tomorrow to check in. Until then."

"Until then, my dear. Tomorrow afternoon, we'll commiserate on how each of our evenings went."

AT SEVEN O'CLOCK SHARP, the doorman informed me that Marcus had arrived and was on his way up.

Tonight should be interesting, I thought as I walked toward the bank of elevators in the foyer. I assessed myself in front of the large mirror on the wall opposite them.

And who is this? I thought as I looked at the formfitting, glimmering black gown I'd bought at Bergdorf for Maxine's event. Typically, I wore Chanel suits, so I was unused to seeing myself in evening wear, let alone something as sexy and glamorous as this.

Thank goodness I work hard to keep thin, because this gown conceals nothing, I thought.

I turned to look at my exposed back, which was a bold, daring choice, even for me.

But it works.

After I did a final check of my makeup and hair, which were on point thanks to Bernie, the middle elevator dinged, and its steel doors whisked open.

When I turned around, there stood Marcus, with his

hands in his pockets and a grin on his face. "Jesus," he said as he looked at me. "Barbara—wow."

He left the elevator and approached me as I soaked him in. He was wearing a beautifully tailored black tux, a stainless steel Rolex Cosmograph Daytona watch on his left wrist, and a masculine pair of Tom Ford leather loafers with a cap toe.

I thought he looked beyond handsome.

And sexy.

"You look beautiful," he said as he walked over to give me a light kiss on the lips. "Would you turn for me? So I can see the rest of the gown?"

"Of course."

I twirled twice for him, and each time I did, I was delighted by his surprised expression when he saw how the gown revealed my back.

"Do you like?" I asked.

"I've never seen you in anything like this," he said. "You look stunning. Can I see the back again?"

I complied.

"There's only one thing I'd change," he said.

That surprised me.

"What is that?"

"It's a minor detail, but I think I've got the fix for it."

"What are you talking about?"

"How do you feel about these?"

When I turned to him, I watched him remove two velvet bags from his pants pocket.

"When I saw these at Van Cleef, I thought of you," he said as his eyes met mine.

I looked down as he removed a piece of jewelry I

recognized at once—Jennifer had nearly purchased the collection herself a little over a month ago. First was the Folie des Prés necklace, an elegant showpiece made of white gold and adorned with hundreds of round and pear-shaped gems. There were diamonds of course, but there also was a mix of pink and mauve sapphires, all of which had been skillfully set to look like delicate wild-flowers. When he removed the matching bracelet and the drop earrings from the other bag, I knew I was looking at least $500,000 worth of jewelry.

"When the manager confirmed these are wildflowers, that sealed the deal for me," he said. "I bought the set because you are *my* wildflower. Can I put the necklace on you?"

"Marcus, I don't know what to say."

"Just say yes," he said. "But first I'll need to remove the necklace you're wearing. Can I?"

When I gave him my back, he took off my necklace, placed it on the table in front of me, and lifted the Folie des Prés necklace over my head and fastened it as I watched in the mirror.

The stones were cool against my neck. The design and the gesture had left me, of all people, nearly speech-less. I touched the necklace with my fingertips and thought it was perfection.

"My gift to you," he said. "Now for the earrings and bracelet."

Moments later, when I was wearing the complete collection, my eyes started to well with tears as I looked at myself. I quickly tried to blink them away, but Marcus saw them—and even though I loathed showing emotion, I decided in this moment, I shouldn't. Words were cheap. Let him see for himself what this gift means to me.

"Marcus, they're beautiful."

He placed his warm hand against the center of my bare back.

"I'm glad you like them," he said. "Martini?"

"Yes, but this first," I said as I reached up to give him a kiss on the lips. He was so tall, I was grateful I was wearing four-inch heels. When his arms wrapped around my waist, he pressed my body against his and held me for a moment. "Thank you," I said after I kissed him again. "I've never received anything so extravagant."

"Never?"

"Not once."

"Then I'll need to change that."

My eyes widened.

"Marcus, that's not what I meant. This is beyond generous of you. You don't have to give me anything ever again—and I mean that."

"I know you do. I also know that when you were in love with me, it never was for the money. That's one of the reasons I'm still in love you." He shrugged. "Well, that and the fact that you're the most beautiful, funny, intellectual, and savvy woman I've ever known. Right now, you have hundreds of diamonds glimmering on you, Barbara, but you outshine every one of them. I'm happy you accepted them. There was a part of me that feared you wouldn't."

I could feel myself melting. Bit by bit, my heart was opening to him again. The more time I spent with him, the more I was beginning to accept that maybe love wasn't out of the question for me after all.

And that maybe, just maybe, Marcus and I weren't done with each other quite yet.

"About that martini," I said. "I'd love one."

He reached for my hand and took it in his own.

"You're on. Take me to the bar, and I'll make each of us one."

"Would you?"

"Anything for you."

We started down the hallway that led to the kitchen.

"Alex and Jennifer will be here at eight," I said. "I figured we could go to the party together."

"Why not?" he said. "I enjoy their company. Alex and I particularly get along well."

I recalled a conversation I had with Jennifer when we were selecting gowns at Bergdorf, and the sting I felt was real.

"You do realize when you show up at Maxine's with Marcus on your arm, people are going to lose their minds?" she said.

"Not if we arrive with you and Alex. If we do, all the attention will be on both of you."

"But only for a moment."

"True, but that moment will nevertheless allow me to get inside before they have a chance to question us at all."

Remembering that conversation made me feel ashamed of myself. Did I really need to use their celebrity to keep the focus off Marcus and me? Was I really that desperate for no one to view us as a couple again?

What am I doing? I thought as we stepped into the kitchen. *Any woman who knows Marcus as well as I do would be proud to stand at his side. What is my problem?*

Don't you remember? You're protecting your heart.

But do I still need to?

Do you?

I believe it's time for me to rethink that.

"This is perfect," Marcus said as we walked over to the marble island, on which was everything one needed to make a martini—Lalique martini glasses, Belvedere vodka, olives, vermouth, a silver shaker, and ice in a silver bucket. He looked at me. "Give me a few minutes?"

Or maybe a lifetime, I thought as he started to prepare the drinks. I checked myself when that popped into my head. *There are two hearts on the line here. Before I get ahead of myself and say something I might regret, I need to pay attention to every moment I have with him, continue to sit with my emotions, and give this more time before we take it to the next level.*

What's the next level?

Being a couple again.

Is that what you want?

I looked at the dimples in Marcus's cheeks, admired the broadness of his shoulders, and felt his presence filling the room with ease. It was good having him here. Hell, it felt *right* having him here. Now that he was back in my life, I no longer seemed so desperately alone in this apartment.

Answer the question, Barbara.

Maybe I will after tonight . . .

SEVENTEEN
MARCUS

Is she starting to come around? I wondered as I made our martinis. *She seems different tonight. More accessible. Or am I just hoping that's the case? I never know when it comes to her.*

After I poured vodka, a touch of vermouth, and ice into the shaker, I looked up and studied her as I smashed the contents together. She was standing at one of the kitchen's enormous windows overlooking a city whose glimmer had nothing on her. Her back was to me.

And so was her ass, which was perfection, especially in *that* gown, which left little to the imagination.

If we didn't have to go to Maxine's party tonight, I'd drop everything, take her into her bedroom, undress her, carry her over to her bed, and run my tongue all over her body.

But that would have to wait until later. Meanwhile, my cock needed to get in line because after imagining Barbara writhing on the bed as I plunged my tongue inside her? It was rock hard.

She accepted the gifts, I thought with a concealed smile as I continued to shake the container. *I didn't think she would, but she did, and that gives me hope because they came from my heart. I believe part of the reason she teared up is because she knew that. A cynic would think I was trying to buy her love, but no one buys Barbara Blackwell's love, and I have zero interest in even trying. If she falls in love with me a second time, it will be because she believes she can trust me with her heart again. And if that happens? It's something I'll never take for granted.*

"Here we go," I said as I lifted the cover off the shaker. I stabbed three olives with a toothpick for her, did the same for me, and then placed each of them in the martini glasses before filling them with the cold liquid.

She walked over to me and looked at the drinks.

"Is there anything sexier than a martini glass?"

I handed her one.

"You."

"And now I look as if I was fishing for a compliment."

"But you weren't, because that's not you." I picked up my own cocktail. "Cheers, Barbara."

She touched her glass to mine.

"Cheers, Marcus."

After we sipped our drinks, she smiled at me.

"Perfection."

"What are you looking forward to tonight?" I asked.

"Certainly spending the evening with you, Alex, and Jennifer," she said. "Other than that, it all depends on who's there. You never know who's going to try to push my buttons, Marcus."

"Somebody will," I said.

She raised her eyebrows.

"And how awful for them if they do."

———

WHEN ALEX and Jennifer arrived at eight, Barbara and I went to the foyer to greet them.

"Oh," Jennifer said when she left the elevator in her own knockout of a gown. "Barbara, that dress is amazing."

"What she said," Alex seconded after he came over to shake my hand. Our eyes met. "Lucky you."

I nodded.

"Right?"

"And those jewels," Jennifer said. "You and I admired them about a month ago at Van Cleef. Did you go back and buy them for yourself? They cost a fortune."

"Actually, they're from Marcus," she said. "Earlier tonight, he gifted them to me."

Jennifer looked over at me.

"You nailed it, Marcus."

"Thank you, Jennifer."

"Would anyone like a drink?" Barbara asked. "Or should we leave?"

"I vote to go early so that we can leave early," Alex said.

"I'm with Alex," I said.

"It's cold outside," Barbara said. "Where are your coats?"

"They're in the limousine," Alex said. "If there's a line at Maxine's, we'll put them on. But before we leave, can we tour your apartment? I haven't seen it yet."

"Of course," Barbara said. "But let's be quick about it, because I'm with you and Marcus." She glanced at me. "I don't want to be out too late either."

I smiled at her.

After a brief tour of the apartment, we left the building, stepped into the limousine Alex and Jennifer had waiting for us at the curbside, and headed to Maxine and Bill's party—with Barbara's hand held firmly in mine.

EIGHTEEN
BARBARA

When we pulled up to the Witherhouse's mansion on the corner of Fifth and Seventy-Ninth Streets, people were starting to arrive in their Rolls-Royces and limousines, some were on the sidewalk posing for the paps, and a line of others were at the front door waiting to get inside.

The building itself was nothing short of magnificent.

It was one of Manhattan's few remaining mansions, and I knew that as long as the Witherhouses owned it, it wouldn't be torn down to allow for new development. They had *that* kind of old money. Nothing would roll over them or this house while they were still alive, and regardless of how much I hated that they were a couple of snobs, I respected them for protecting a landmark as special at this.

"It's amazing, isn't it?" Marcus said. "Especially at night. Maxine turned on all the lights in an effort to make it glow, and she pulled it off." He shook his head. "It's exceptional."

"You should make them an offer and buy it for yourself," I said to him.

He turned to me with a bemused smile on his face. "What would I do with twenty-seven rooms on six floors?"

"Get your exercise in by jogging through them each morning?"

"Actually, that's not a bad idea," Jennifer said. "You could sweat it out throughout the house."

"I prefer fresh air."

"And yet you live in Manhattan," Alex said.

Marcus laughed at that.

"Touché," he said.

"Are we ready?" Jennifer asked.

"I'm ready," I said.

Alex and Marcus said the same.

"The paps are there, Barbara," Jennifer said to me. "I know you hate to be photographed by them, so why don't Alex and I go first? They'll hammer us with questions, and while they do, you and Marcus can slip by them and go to the back of the line. Does that work?"

My heart pulled when she asked me that question because now it felt so wrong.

It's not her fault, I thought. *She doesn't know my feelings have changed.*

I gave her a discreet wink, which I hoped told her everything I couldn't say to her now.

"Thank you, Jennifer," I said. "But I'd like to be photographed with Marcus. In fact, it's been too long since we were photographed together."

Marcus squeezed my knee.

"Are you sure?" he asked me. "They're going to ask us questions."

"Let them."

"*Personal* questions. We discussed this a few days ago —remember?"

"I remember."

"You had concerns about that."

"I did then."

"You don't now?"

"If they want to ask if we're dating again, let them."

"And if they ask if we're a couple?"

Alex cleared his throat.

"Jennifer?" he said. "Why don't we step outside for a second?"

"I was just thinking that."

When we were alone, I looked at Marcus. "How do you want to answer that question?"

"You already know—I want to tell them and the world that we are a couple again. I want to shout it from the rooftops. But we haven't discussed where we stand—"

"So tell them that," I said.

He looked at me—stunned.

"That we're a couple?"

I placed the palm of my hand against his cheek.

"That we're a couple who is very much in love."

"Are you serious?"

"Would I say any of that if I wasn't?"

When his eyes brightened, so did mine. And for once, I didn't blink my tears away because I didn't care if he saw my facade crack as the walls I'd built between us started to tumble down. I didn't have the energy or the desire to do this anymore. I couldn't keep trying to convince myself that I didn't love him when I did. It was too much work to keep denying it over and over again. From myself and especially from him.

Fear had tried its best to keep us apart, but tonight? Fear failed.

"I love you," I said.

"You do?"

"I do. I'm so grateful you came back into my life. And I want to apologize that it took me time to get my head on straight. I just needed to be sure that this time it would work out."

"It will," he said. "I believe in us. I always have."

"I want to kiss you, but I'd destroy Bernie's hair and makeup if I did."

"After the party then?"

I nodded.

"Tonight, I want you to make love to me like you've never made love to me before," I said.

"You don't have to ask me twice."

I motioned toward the door.

"Shall we?"

He opened the door, stepped out of the limousine, and turned to offer me his hand.

"Let's do this," he said.

And we did.

With Jennifer and Alex leading the way, we all went through the motions of being photographed by the paps. Jennifer and I were asked who we were wearing, Alex was hammered with multiple questions about news relating to Wenn, and just when I thought everyone had forgotten that Marcus and I were once a couple, the questions about why I was here with him suddenly started to come.

With a vengeance.

Amid the explosions of light emerging from the cameras, Marcus took control of the situation and answered only once. He reached for my hand and simply said to them, "Barbara Blackwell is the love of my life. We're a couple again, we're deeply in love, and I'm thrilled to say we're very happy."

More questions came, but for Marcus? That was it. With my hand still in his, we joined Alex and Jennifer in the line of people now moving steadily into the mansion, and soon we were inside.

But not before Alex and Jennifer congratulated us.

"This is cause for celebration," Jennifer said as we approached the seemingly endless reception line. She looked at Marcus and me. "And we're going to do that tonight."

"Bring it on," Marcus said. "I've waited too long for this."

"To be honest, so have we," Alex said. "We're just happy it finally happened."

Fifteen minutes later, after Alex and Jennifer finished speaking with Maxine and her husband, Bill, it was our turn.

And what a turn it was . . .

NINETEEN
MARCUS

"Marcus!" Maxine called out as Barbara and I approached her and Bill. "And Barbara! My goodness. Now the party has *really* begun."

"If that's the case, our work here is done," Barbara said to me beneath her breath.

"Which means I can get you into bed sooner rather than later."

"Just say the word and I'm naked."

Don't laugh, I thought. *Keep it together.*

"Hello, Bill," I said as we approached them. "Maxine. It's good to see you. Thank you for having us."

"I'm so happy you're here, Marcus," Maxine said after she clocked Barbara's necklace and earrings with a swift sidelong glance. "And especially with Barbara. This has to mean you're a couple again. Tell me it's so."

"It is so," I said.

"Well, that's just fabulous," Maxine said. "You two make such an interesting couple."

"Interesting?"

"Oh yes—and glamorous. *Très chic!*"

"Thank you, Maxine."

Maxine was a slight blonde in her late sixties, but given how vibrant and youthful she looked, one would question whether she'd even reached fifty. Bill, on the other hand, was a tall, distinguished-looking man with a shock of white hair who looked every bit his age—midseventies. And because of that, his age actually exposed an unwanted truth about Maxine. Everyone knew they'd been married fifty years. And with him standing so close to her, the deep lines on his face only underscored the fact that she had none.

Which is what's really interesting, I thought.

"Your gown is to die for, Barbara," Maxine said. "*Très élégant!* Who made it for you?"

"Ralph," Barbara said. "But it wasn't made for me, Maxine. Instead, it was just tailored to me."

"You got *that* off the rack? My goodness—where?"

"Bergdorf."

"Oh," she said. "Bergdorf. An institution, yes, but for me? Also a distant memory. Ever since I decided to commit to everything haute couture, I haven't been there in years."

"I see," Barbara said as she turned her head to the side and looked at Maxine's red sequined gown. "And yours? You know I love a gown with a sleeveless, one-shoulder neckline—we talked about that the last time I saw you. Do you remember? You were wearing a similar gown."

"I was?"

"You were, but it's fine. In fact, I'm likely the only

one who has noticed. Now, as for this one, I'm assuming it's Dior? It has to be."

"It is Dior," she said coolly. "Very good, Barbara. So fashion savvy. I bought it off a model two weeks ago in Paris."

"So in reality you bought it off *her* rack?"

"Always so quick," Maxine said with a dismissive little laugh. "Now you must tell me about your necklace and earrings. They are the *real* exclamation points in the room."

I watched Barbara raise her right arm.

"Let's not forget about the matching bracelet."

Maxine looked at the bracelet for a moment before her eyes flashed up to meet Barbara's. "Let's not. Cartier?"

"Van Cleef. They're a gift from Marcus."

"Of course they are, darling. I can only imagine how thrilled you are that Marcus is so generous."

Before Barbara could respond to that, I got in front of it.

"We should go," I said. "We're holding up the line."

"It's so funny," Maxine said. "First, I hear from friends that Barbara has moved to a swanky new apartment on Billionaire's Row—and now it appears as if she's dressing like one."

"Style does take money," Barbara said. "Just not billions, Maxine."

Get these two away from each other now.

"Anyway," I said as I placed my hand against Barbara's bare back. "Alex and Jennifer are waiting for us, so we should probably join them."

"Of course," Bill said.

"Have a successful party," I said as we started to move away from them. "And thank you again for having us."

"I'm sure we'll see you again once we can mingle," Maxine said. "In the meantime, the bar is just upstairs in the ballroom. Barbara, I know you love your martinis, so have one or three on me. Enjoy!"

"She's an awful human being," Barbara said when we were out of earshot.

"And yet you handled her with ease."

She glanced up at me.

"That's because of you," she said. "Thank you for moving us along, because there's no telling how sharp my tongue would have become if you hadn't."

"Enough of Maxine," I said.

"Agreed." She looked around the massive foyer, which had been tastefully decorated for the party. A huge, twinkling Christmas tree dominated the center of the room, which was teaming with people taking the dramatic, bifurcated staircase just ahead of us to the second floor ballroom. "You know?" she said. "After that little exchange, I think I would like a martini. Shall we?"

"Absolutely."

But when we reached the second floor, which had been beautifully decorated for the holidays and featured an eleven-piece orchestra playing Tchaikovsky's "December: Christmas" at the far end of the room, we unexpectedly came face-to-face with a couple I knew she never wanted to see, especially at an event such as this.

It was her ex-husband, Charles, and his second wife,

Rita, each of whom I recognized only because Barbara had once shown me photographs of them.

"Look at her," Barbara had said at the time while pointing at one particularly unattractive picture of Rita. "A whore with a horsey face. I bet Charles feeds her cubes of sugar."

And I bet this could turn into a shitshow, I thought as she gripped my hand. *Especially since they're about ten feet away from us—and looking aghast.*

"Never mind them," I said. "Let's just go to the bar and order a drink."

"And allow them to think I'm a coward because I ignored them?" she said. "You know me better than that, so allow me to apologize for everything that's about to take place now . . ."

TWENTY

BARBARA

"Well, well, well," I said as I looked at my former husband and his slut of a wife. "I wasn't expecting to see party filler so quickly, but here you two are, so apparently I was wrong."

"We're hardly party filler, Barbara," Charles said.

"But aren't you?" I asked. "The massacre that took place here four years ago must have taken its toll on Maxine's gilded guest list if she was forced to fill this joint by sending you two an invite."

"You know that's bullshit," he said.

"And yet I know nothing," I said. "Either way, all I can say is this, Charles. With you and the glue factory here, Maxine has placed a stain on her reputation."

"The *what* factory?" Charles said.

I rolled my eyes at him.

"You're such an old, aging cliché, Charles—you really are. In the heated throes of your midlife crisis, first you cheated on me, then you married a woman half your age, and now it's clear you're having difficulty with your hearing. It's sad, really, but what's worse is that your hair has become so unnaturally black, it's no secret you've succumbed to the kitchen sink dye job." I raised my eyebrows. "Is Botox next? Filler? I can only imagine the pincushion your face is about to become."

Before he could clap back, I looked over at Rita, whose horsey face had flushed red with anger.

"Why do you stay with him when he won't even buy you a decent gown?" I asked her. "Everything about that gold metallic mess you're wearing screams either Bloomingdale's, Century 21, or maybe even Macy's. Charles is so cheap, it could be any one of them."

"Why are you so hateful?" she asked.

"Because she's a bitch," Charles said. "She always has been."

I was about to go for his jugular when Marcus stepped forward and cut between us. He was so tall and built, he towered over Charles, who was a good six inches shorter.

"Call her that again, and you'll have my fist in your face," he said to Charles. "Got it?"

"It's time for you to leave, Charles," Alex said when he and Jennifer appeared in the crowd. "If you don't, you'll also have me to contend with. Choose."

"We just got here, Alex."

"Doesn't matter," Marcus said. "Those are your choices."

"She came for me first!"

"Is a woman too much for you to handle, Charles?"

Jennifer asked. "Because if that's the case, allow me to quote Barbara—*j'adore* it." She motioned toward the staircase behind her. "That's your way out of this situation," she said. "I suggest you take it."

"To hell with this," Rita said to Charles in a low voice. She grabbed hold of his hand. "We should leave before people start to talk. Neither of us wants that."

"And yet they're already talking," I said to them as they started to walk away. "Toodles, darlings. Do your best to pretend nothing is being said about you, and enjoy the quiet ride home."

"I APOLOGIZE FOR THAT," I said to Marcus, Alex, and Jennifer when Charles and Rita were gone. "Whenever I run into them, which thankfully is rare, it triggers me."

"Why wouldn't it?" Jennifer said. "How he treated you at the end of your marriage was beyond hurtful. Sometimes that kind of pain and betrayal never goes away, which is why you lash out. I get it. I just wish Alex and I had been here to witness everything that was said."

"It wasn't my proudest moment," I admitted. *And yet I chose to do it in front of Marcus, of all people,* I thought. *What is he going to think of me now? A woman scorned? An unhinged shrew?*

Thankfully, it didn't take me long to find out.

"I thought you were brilliant," he said.

I looked up at him.

"Marcus—"

"You were," he said. "And Jennifer is right. My ex cheated on me, so I know how it feels. It does hurt. And sometimes you want to hurt them back." He put his hand on my shoulder. "You were just being human, Barbara. There's nothing to apologize for."

"All of you are being very generous."

"We're just telling you the truth," Alex said. "Charles deserved whatever you said to him and probably a hell of a lot more." He clapped his hands once. "But I'm not about to let him ruin our evening, so why don't we leave all that BS behind and have a cocktail? I think we could use one."

"Oh look," I said. "Something I won't argue with."

Alex laughed at that before he turned to Marcus. "Join me at the bar? I could use another pair of hands to bring back the drinks."

"You've got it."

Before he left with Alex, Marcus gently squeezed my shoulder.

"I love him," Jennifer said as she watched them move into the crowd. "He's so right for you."

"He is," I agreed.

"And you're in love with him again."

"I am."

"How does it feel?"

"Surreal but in the best way," I said as I looked at her. "I thought we were finished."

"Marcus had other ideas."

"Thank God he did."

"He fought hard to win you back."

"He did," I said. "And I plan to make sure he never regrets it."

She looked over my shoulder and started to smile.

"Someone's coming our way," she said.

Before I could ask who, an unmistakable voice rang out in the crowd.

"The cookies!" I heard Epifania Zapopa say at my back. "Finally! I been looking the everywhere for the you!"

"She should lift the night," Jennifer said to me.

As inappropriate and bawdy as she could be, I'd nevertheless warmed to Epifania over the years, so much so that I now considered her a friend. In her own unhinged way, she could be the unexpected life of the party, especially if given the right platform and enough tequila laid bare on an empty stomach.

When I turned to her, I was pleased by what I saw. No longer did she wear the revealing sort of trash she had favored when we first met. Instead, after I decided to school her on fashion—and especially after she started to date the uberwealthy and handsome Rudman Cross—she dressed beautifully. Elegantly. And tonight was no exception. As she ribboned through the crowd with an excited smile on her face, I could see she was wearing a black column gown by Jason Wu. With her long, thick brown hair curling around her shoulders, her makeup on point, and the diamonds glimmering at her neck, ears, fingers, and wrists, I thought this might be the best I'd ever seen her.

She looked that stunning. That polished. Until, of course, she opened her mouth.

"*Heyzeus Cristo*," she said when she came upon us. "Thees place remind me of me Rudsy's package—it packed so tight, I think it gonna pop!"

"There's an image," Jennifer said.

"And a good one, right? Now give me the kisses. Both of you. Kiss, kiss, kiss. That the right. It what we reech people do—kiss the cheek, sometimes the ass."

"I kiss no one's ass, Epifania," I said.

"Lady, I get it, OK? One, you didn't grow up on a fucking banana leaf—I did. Two, you didn't come to thees country in a rubber boat filled with fifty squabbling relatives—I did. I only kiss the ass when I forget I got Chuckie's five hundred million when he die. Sue me."

"I despise litigation."

"You hate the lesbians?"

"That's not what I said."

"Good, because I thought your daughter one."

"Alexa is not a lesbian."

"Really? Because Daniella told me she rolls her own tampons, which I thought was pretty damn butch."

"Daniella has said many questionable things about her sister, but they're in a better place now."

For a moment, she looked shocked.

"Well sheet—when they die?"

"That's not what I meant."

"But you said they in better place."

"I—oh never mind."

"They don't argue as much," Jennifer said. "That's why they're in a better place, Epifania."

I need to change this subject now.

"Where is Rudman, Epifania?" I asked.

"Well, he not in a better place, that for the sure." She motioned around the ballroom. "I don't know," she said. "He somewhere in here, probably talking business like he always does."

"You know," Jennifer said, "you two have been seeing each other for years. Isn't it time for you to seal the deal?"

"What deal? The only deal I have with Rudsy is that I've agreed to stay ready so I don't have to get ready."

"Sorry?"

"You know—for the butt bang."

"The butt bang?"

"*Heyzeus Cristo,* Yennifer! You know. Taking it up the hoo-ha!"

"I am so not talking about anal sex," Jennifer said.

"That's curious," I said. "Because right now, everyone around us is. But, please, do carry on."

"What the hell you talking about, lady?" she said to Jennifer.

"I'm asking if you're going to get *married.*"

"Married? That what thees about? If it is, we no getting married."

"But why?"

"Because the moment you put a ring on it, the sexy times die. Everyone know that."

"They haven't for Alex and me."

"Who happens to be coming our way now," I said to them. "With Marcus. They have our martinis."

"Marcus?" Epifania said. "Why he here? I thought you dump him?"

"We're back together."

"You are? And you no tell me?"

"It's very recent," I said. "But let's not discuss that now. Just be yourself around him, OK?"

As they approached us, Jennifer and Epifania turned to greet them.

"Marcus!" Epifania said. "It been the years and the years!"

"It's good to see you, Epifania," Marcus said with a smile as he handed me my martini. He checked to see if Epifania had a drink, which she didn't. "Would you like my martini?" he asked her. "I don't mind getting another one for myself."

"Oh!" she said. "Oh no. No, no, no."

"Are you sure?"

"I am sure," she said. And then she lowered her voice. "For good reason, I'm sure."

He looked at me, I raised my eyebrows, and then he looked back at Epifania—confused.

"I'm not following," he said.

"Then let me tell you," she said. "If you go back so soon, people will think you're an alcoholic. And then everyone will start the talking and the tittering. They gonna say, 'That Marcus Koch is one stone-cold drunk.' They gonna say, 'Someone needs a new leever.' And they even gonna say, 'Don't smoke around him—he like gasoline!' That's just how these motherfuckers are."

"I see," he said. "Well, thank you, Epifania. I hadn't thought of that."

"My pleasure, papi."

"Papi?" I said to her.

"Lady, why you sound so surprised?" she said. "Just like me Rudsy, Marcus is a total papi. He tall, he strong, he the sexy good looking, he got the silvery hair, and he the reech! You should start calling him Big Papi or Big Daddy—whatever—because it true."

Alex turned to Marcus.

"From now on, I am so calling you Big Papi."

"Just hope I can say the same to you when you're my age."

"Anyway," Epifania said. "I should go. Me Rudsy might need me to save him from someone awful." She looked at Jennifer. "Like that *perra*, Tootie Staunton-Miller."

"Please don't say that woman's name around me," Jennifer warned her.

"Why not? She here."

"She is? Are you sure?"

"Sure I sure—I see her while looking for you."

"Fantastic," Jennifer said.

"You can take her," Epifania said. "So if she come for you, I say you smash her into leetle bitty bits of nothing and have the good times when you do so." She looked at me. "Rudsy and I excited about your Christmas Eve party," she said. "Gracias for the invitation."

"It's my pleasure, Epifania." I raised my martini to her. "After all, with you there, I won't need to spike the eggnog."

"What that mean?"

"It's a compliment," I said. "Now give us a kiss, go find Rudman, and tell him we also look forward to seeing him at the party."

"*Besos!*" she said before she made her way into the crowd. "*Besos y abrazos!* We see you in a week."

When I was certain she couldn't hear me, I looked at Marcus, Alex, and Jennifer.

"Which should give all of us enough time to recover from that."

TWENTY-ONE
MARCUS

An hour later, after catching up with some mutual friends and stealing a few discreet moments to share a kiss with Barbara, the orchestra started playing "Moon River," and I knew at once what I had to do.

I offered my hand to her.

"Dance with me?" I asked.

She looked over at the dance floor, which was filled with people coming together and embracing each other as the song began.

"I'd love to," she said as she took my hand.

When I led her to the dance floor, I was aware of heads turning to look at us as we began to waltz—and the surprise I saw in their eyes told me it was now clear to everyone that Barbara and I were back together.

I did it, I thought as we moved to the music. *I won her back.*

"Don't leave me just yet," she said.

I looked at her.

"Leave you?" I said. "Barbara, if you'll have me, I never plan on leaving you."

She smiled at that. "That's good to know," she said. "But the reason I said that is because a moment ago, it felt as if you were a million miles away."

"Oh that," I said as we turned with the rest of the crowd. "I was in my head."

"What's in there?"

"A lot of things," I said. "Gratitude. Relief. My love for you. How happy I am to be back in your life. How happy I am that you gave us a second chance." I held her closer to me and ran my left hand down the length of her bare back. "You know, all the things that are connected to my heart."

"Thank you for coming back for me," she said.

"I'm just sorry it took so long."

"And I'm still sorry I didn't trust any of it when you did."

"You had your reasons, Barbara—valid ones."

"I'm just happy it's all behind us," she said and then she looked seriously at me. "Not every man is Charles, Marcus. You taught me that. I'm sorry what he did to me affected me to the point that I almost pushed you away. I think I hate that the most. All the hurt, anger, and fear that man left me with was greater than I knew."

"But you've faced that now."

"Only because you persisted."

"Do you feel you've moved beyond it?"

"For the most part, yes."

"What's the other part?"

She winked at me. "I couldn't give a damn about

Charles, but that doesn't mean I'll ever stop enjoying it when I have the opportunity to tear him down. What took place between us earlier tonight was fun for me but hell for him, and I'm living for it. Better yet, I'm not ashamed to admit it."

"I get it," I said. "The problem for me is that while I can dream of shaming my ex in public, if I actually did so, she'd slap me with a restraining order."

The song ended.

"Best not to have that on your record," Barbara said as we left the floor. When something caught her eye, she suddenly stopped. I followed her gaze to none other than Tootie Staunton-Miller and her husband, Addy, who were literally within feet of Jennifer.

"Her back is to them," Blackwell said. "She's about to be hijacked by that shrew, and she doesn't even know it. Where is Alex?"

I looked around the room but didn't see him.

"I'm not sure," he said. "Restroom?"

"It's possible."

Either way, I reached for her hand.

"Why don't we go over and have her back?" I said. "I know Tootie and Addy. Addy is great, but Tootie snipes from the side. She likes to sting with her words. And you just happen to be one of the few people I know who can destroy her if she gets out of line."

"I feel seen," Barbara said with a smirk as we started toward the group. "Let's see what's about to be said. Jennifer can hold her own against her, but who knows? Tootie is only approaching to cause trouble. If she decides to go too low, perhaps I'll need to intervene . . ."

TWENTY-TWO
BARBARA

The ballroom was so packed, Marcus and I didn't reach Jennifer until it was too late—Tootie and Addy were just about to speak with her. And so instead of interrupting them, we decided to hang back and listen to see if she needed me at all.

"Jennifer," Tootie said in that lilting, condescending voice of hers. "Hellohoware?"

Startled, Jennifer turned to face her. And when she did? She didn't seem at all happy to be looking at Tootie, who nevertheless offered Jennifer her hand.

And how will she deal with this? I wondered as I watched.

"I'm sorry, Tootie," she said after a moment. "But I can't."

"You can't what?"

"Shake your hand."

"It's a hand, Jennifer. I mean, my goodness. Why ever not?"

"Because it's yours?"

"Excuse me?"

"Well, that and monkeypox," Jennifer said. "I have a husband and a young son I need to protect, and you might be a carrier. For their safety alone, I'm afraid I can't take the risk of touching your skin."

"You think I have monkeypox?"

"Tootie, I don't know what you have or don't have. That said, if you were so casually willing to shake *my* hand, I have to wonder how many other hands you've touched tonight." She shrugged. "I think it's safe to assume you've shaken plenty, which to me means you're a high-risk individual. We all need to be careful, don't you agree?"

Tootie, who was sixtyish but looked fiftyish, smiled tightly at Jennifer when she dropped her hand. She was an attractive woman with blonde hair that just touched her shoulders. She wore understated jewels at her throat, wrists, and fingers, and she had chosen a black gown I had to admit was . . . pretty. Her formfitting dress could betray more mature curves, but Tootie Staunton-Miller looked trim and terrific. She also reeked of class and old money and had the kind of white privilege that likely made her believe she was immune to such a low-rent virus as monkeypox.

"While I think all of this is ridiculous, Jennifer, we'll err on the side of safety for you," she said. "And especially if it's only to settle your nerves, because I have to imagine just being here tonight has you on edge, darling. Am I right? After all, it was just four years ago when that madman Stephen Rowe tried to have you and Alex gunned down right here at poor Maxine's mansion."

"People died that night, Tootie—including friends of mine. And you're being flippant about it?"

"Actually, I'm being factual."

"No, you aren't. What you're being is what you've always been to me—a bitch."

"Oh dear," I said beneath my breath. "She's never gone that far."

I watched Jennifer look at Addy, whom I knew she adored. "I'm sorry if I offended you, Addy. But I'm beyond tired of your wife's behavior. I don't know what her issue is with me, but after all these years, I'm officially sick of her coming for me." She turned to Tootie, who had a bemused, self-satisfied look on her face.

She wants Jennifer to look unhinged, I thought. *In front of everyone. And she's winning.*

"And for what?" Jennifer said. "What's the reason, Tootie? Are you threatened by me?"

"From a woman who hails from the hog farms of Maine?" she said. "Hardly, darling. In fact, no one threatens me."

Really? I thought as I reached for Marcus's hand and we started to walk over to them. *No one? Let's see about that, Tootie. Show me what you've got.*

"Did somebody say bitch?" I asked as Marcus and I stood on either side of Jennifer. I caught the surprised look on her face when she saw us, but I knew better than to acknowledge it. Instead, I kept my attention laser-focused on Tootie. "Because if you want one, Tootie, here I am."

"And you're correct," Tootie said with a smile. "There's

no question that person would be *you*, Barbara." She raised her chin and narrowed her eyes. "I remember when you used to come to these events with Charles. It's only because of his contacts that you were allowed access into *our* world but then the divorce struck—and suddenly the invitations just stopped arriving in the mail, didn't they?" She shook her head. "My, how that must have stung."

"Not as much as being accused of having monkeypox at Maxine's big Christmas mixer," I said. "Because that had to be brutal for you to hear, Tootie. I mean, my goodness—just imagine how many people overheard it and are discussing it with others now."

Before she could respond, I looked at Addy, whose irritation with his wife was beyond apparent.

"Addy, I hate to put you on the spot, but perhaps you could shed some light on why your wife clearly detests Jennifer," I said. "I have my own ideas, of course, most of which come down to Tootie's raging jealousy over Jennifer's beauty, intelligence, poise, and power. But I don't have your insight. Would you be willing to share it?"

When he turned to me, I met his gaze with my own. I'd known Addy for years. When I was with Charles, we were actually quite friendly despite his marriage to Tootie, who also had never liked me.

He knows I know he's gay, I thought. *He also knows I've never judged him for it. Is his fear of being exposed the reason he tolerates Tootie? Does he stay married to her because he's certain she would out him the moment he left her? But that doesn't make sense because he isn't a stupid man. He must be aware that everyone knows he's in the closet, so why does he stay?*

As the silence stretched between us, a possible reason came to me.

It could be because he knows that when it comes to society, there are some things you never say or admit out of fear of becoming blacklisted.

"Addy?" I pressed. "Any insight would help."

"Leave my husband out of this," Tootie said.

"Why?" I asked. "Because he knows too much?"

"No, Barbara. Because however I behave around anyone is on me—not him. He knows that. He also knows that my disdain for interlopers like you, Jennifer, and so many others is part of my DNA. I want all of you out of our lives. We're a closed society with no room for any of you."

"And yet here we are," I said as Alex joined Jennifer's side. "Invited by Maxine herself."

"I never said my work was done, Barbara. But one day it will be, and when that day arrives?" She linked arms with Addy. "We'll finally be able to live in peace."

"Peace," Addy scoffed as he removed his wife's arm from his. "I think I'm going to start enjoying some of that now, because I can't be part of this anymore. It's too cruel, it's too embarrassing, and it's not right."

Confused, Tootie just looked at him.

"What are you saying?"

Addy turned to Tootie.

"That I'm divorcing you."

As shocking as his statement was, I had to give it to Tootie for not flinching.

"No, you aren't, Addy." She laughed. "Don't be silly."

"I know you're going to try to ruin me for making that decision, but so be it. It's what you do, Tootie, but I'll be fine. Over the past two months, I've put things into motion that you know nothing about."

"Such as?"

"A new apartment of my own," he said. "Which I have to say is fabulous. I've also spoken to our friends, the majority of whom support me and who couldn't give a damn if I'm gay. In fact, they're just happy I'm finally going to live my authentic life."

"Bullshit," Tootie said.

"It's none of that and you know it," Addy said. "Times have changed. People are more accepting. And since I still have some life left in me yet, I'm glad I finally found the courage to make the decision that will forever get me the hell away from you."

"Bravo," Jennifer said.

"I second that," I said. "Never forget you have us, Addy. We'll all be here for you." What I didn't say is that I already had Bernie in mind for him. That would have to come later—when things were less tense. Because when I glanced over at Tootie? She was fuming.

"If you go through with any of this, I will destroy you, Addy," she said. "Count on it."

"But don't you see, Tootie?" he said. "I already have. But before I leave, you should know this—after all these years of being married to you, do you really believe I don't have tangible things in my possession that would ruin you? Because I do. And if you think I don't, why don't you come after me and find out what they are?"

He turned to leave but then stopped to deliver one final blow.

"I dare you," he said.

And then, after saying his goodbyes to us, Addison Miller wasn't just released from the trappings of his marriage but also from a sexuality that was never his own.

He was gone, determined to start over and create a new life for himself. As for Tootie? There was no way she was going to stay anywhere near us, so she also left, but this time without saying a word.

"Did that really happen?" Jennifer asked when they were gone.

"Oh, it happened," Alex said. "And good for Addy because that took balls."

"She's going to make life hell for him," Jennifer said.

"Not necessarily," I said. "Addy said he had some *tangible* things he could use against her. She knows what they are, of course. The question is whether we'll ever find out."

"That's up to her," Marcus said.

"And since she's so reckless, I'm ruling none of it out."

"Shall we go?" Alex asked.

"I'm ready," Jennifer said.

"Marcus?" I said.

"Nothing can top that," he said. "Let's go."

Twenty minutes later, Jennifer and Alex dropped us at my place. And five minutes after that?

Marcus was already undressing me in my bedroom.

TWENTY-THREE
BARBARA

The week leading up to the Christmas Eve party was a blur—and not just a happy one. But also a *meaningful* one.

Marcus and I became inseparable. After work, we dined at a handful of restaurants we'd always wanted to try; he spent each night at my apartment; our lovemaking was off the charts; and I eventually suggested we go to his apartment and gather clothes and toiletries for him to keep at my place.

I no longer felt lonely. I no longer missed Daniella and Alexa's daily presence in my home quite as much as I used to. In fact, if anything, I felt loved, appreciated, and understood by a likeminded person who valued me for me.

When I woke each morning, just having Marcus by my side was a gift.

I had begun a new chapter of my life, and I was no longer fighting it. Instead, the more I felt Marcus's love for me—and my love for him—the more I welcomed it.

But now, with the party happening tomorrow, I'd taken the day off to double-check everything before Jennifer and Lisa swung by at noon. Tank's parents had arrived two days ago, and they were staying with him and Lisa. But when Jennifer called me this morning, she told me that Ethel was already up to her old tricks.

"Remember when you and I went to Bergdorf and you suggested that Lisa should fill their bedroom with her zombie novels?" Jennifer said.

"I do."

"Well, she did."

"Did Ethel combust? Because that was the point."

"If only she had. Instead, she 'accidentally' sprayed holy water on those books and destroyed them. Lisa saw the damage this morning, she and Ethel had words, and now she needs your advice. Both of us know you're busy, Barbara, but if there's any way you could see us today, that would be great. We won't take much of your time. Lisa needs us right now. She's upset."

"But what will she do with Harold and Ethel in the meantime?"

"Lisa suggested a new exhibition at the MET to Ethel. It's called *Age of Spirituality: Late Antique and Early Christian Art, Third to Seventh Century.* She's going to drop them there at noon and leave them for a few hours while they think she's doing some last-minute Christmas shopping."

"Well done," I said.

"Do you mind if we come by?"

"Not at all. I'll see you both around noon."

Before they came, I walked around the apartment,

which my friend Thomas—the retired Broadway set designer—had completely transformed with his team over the past three days.

Now, throughout the apartment's many rooms, there were more decorated trees; dozens of smiling snowmen with colorful earmuffs at the entrance to each room; a band of white lights hung above the black Steinway grand piano that now sat in the center of the great room; gorgeous wreaths lined the walls in the galley; and wherever there was a fireplace, it was filled with sparkling gold logs that were lit from within with flickering orange lights. On the mantels? Massive glimmering bows made from round silver ornaments.

I'd asked for elegant, and that's exactly what Thomas had given me. I loved it.

Better yet, so did Marcus.

Now to call the concierge and finalize the menu, I thought as I removed my SlimPhone from my pants pocket.

When I first spoke with him about what I wanted for the party and asked if they had Beluga caviar, I was told they had only Ossetra. But because that would never do for a party I was throwing, I had to hope the utter disappointment I'd laced into my voice had changed all that.

When the concierge answered my call, I was pleased to see that it had.

———

LATER, when Jennifer and Lisa arrived, I took their coats, gave them a quick peek at the apartment's decorations, and then led them to the kitchen. There we'd sit at the island and share a bottle of champagne while Lisa unleashed on her Bible-thumping monster-in-law.

"She's insufferable," Lisa said after I poured each of us a glass.

"I need details," I said.

"And I have plenty."

"Such as? They've only been with you for two days."

"Correction," she said. "Today is the third day."

"Not quite. It's just past noon, so we'll go with two and a half days. But whatever. Jennifer told me what she did to your books, but she didn't tell me how Tank reacted."

"He confronted her," she said.

"Good for Tank. What was said?"

"Ethel told him she was merely in the process of blessing their bedroom with her travel pocket holy water sprinkler when things got out of hand."

"What does that even mean?"

"Oh, you're going to love this," she said. "Apparently, my books triggered some sort of demon within her. Ethel said when she got near them, something came over her, she froze, and then she started to sprinkle the hell out of them until all the water was gone. She intentionally destroyed my books. Tank said if she did it again, he'd use some of that water on her."

"To bless the sick?" I asked. "Or to put her devils to flight?"

"Either one would work for me."

"What else?"

"Her damned audiobooks! After we returned from

dinner on their first night here, Ethel asked if we could all gather in the living room to enjoy a listening session of *God Loves Broken People* (*And Those Who Pretend They're Not*)."

"Oh no, she didn't," Jennifer said.

"I'm being serious."

"The shade of it all."

"Right?"

"Why would you possibly agree to listen to that?" I asked.

"We were trying to be polite, Barbara."

"If that was their first night, I'm assuming she ruined your books later? Likely when they were turning in for the evening?"

"That's right. And then there's the following morning, when she actually asked me of all people to say grace before we had breakfast. The last time I said grace was when I was a kid, so I leaned into that little nugget of gold because I knew it would piss her off."

"What did you say?" I asked.

"Gird your loins, ladies."

"Just tell us," Jennifer said.

Lisa cleared her throat.

"I said—and with a straight face, I might add— 'ABCDEFG, thank you, God, for feeding me.'"

With that, Lisa finished her champagne in one fell swoop, smiled sweetly at us, and held out her glass for me to refill, which I did.

"And how was that received?" I asked.

"Harold laughed," she said. "But Harold gets it. He's the best of Tank, who also laughed."

"And Ethel?"

"Considering the look of abject horror on her face, I think she would have gone all Second Amendment on my ass if she could have found a way to do so. I mean, there was a moment when I thought she was going to cry."

"She'd need feelings to cry, darling."

"There's that."

"How much longer will they be here?" I asked.

"Four more days."

"Then listen to me," I said. "You have two choices. First, you can just suck it up and do your best to get along with her during that time. Or you can have it out with her and deal with four days of *real* hell. Because if you think this is bad, Lisa? Ethel can make it much worse. Trust me on that. Jennifer?"

"I have to agree with the latter," she said. "But I also want to add this—avoid her as much as possible. Talk with Tank. Tell him you need to start taking a few breaks from his mother, which is where I come in. If you need to get away, just text me. Starting today, Alex and I are on vacation until January 2. If Ethel is working your last nerve, you are more than welcome to come to our place and hang with me, Alex, and Aiden. In fact, we'd love it if you did."

"That makes me feel better already," she said. "Thank you, Jennifer."

"It's my pleasure."

"And thank you, Barbara. I know you have a lot on your plate right now. I'm sorry for venting."

"No, no," I said. "Just hearing how you delivered grace gave me life, Lisa. Well played, my dear."

She looked at me.

"Yesterday, Ethel said something about you that's been bothering me."

"About *me*? Pray tell."

"She said it in passing."

"What is it?"

"While I was making coffee, she began speaking to Harold. In a voice I was clearly meant to hear, she said, 'Wouldn't it be awful of me if I foiled Barbara's party the way she tried to destroy my day at Mitchell and Lisa's wedding?'"

"She *what*?" Jennifer said.

"There's more," I said. "When she said that, Harold called her out. He said, 'That wouldn't be very Christian of you, Ethel.' And then Ethel said, 'True, but that's what the confessional is for, Harold. To remain in good favor with the Lord, all I need to do is admit everything to Father Harvey when we return home.'"

"Interesting," I said. "I wonder what Ethel would do to try to ruin the party?"

"I don't know," Lisa said. "But I think she's coming for you, Barbara. That one forgets nothing. And worse for you, she forgives no one. I don't know if she has the balls to take you on, but I still needed you to be aware that it's a possibility."

"Have you shared any of this with Tank?"

"I have."

"What are his thoughts?"

"He said he's going to watch her like a hawk. If he

thinks she's up to something, he believes he can shut her down quickly without anyone knowing."

"And on the off chance he fails?"

"If that happens, I say you go for the jugular, humiliate her publicly, and then throw her ass out of your apartment. I'll feel bad for Harold, who naturally will leave with her. But I can tell you this—Tank and I won't be joining them. We'll be staying put."

"I appreciate that," I said. "But I also need to consider Marcus. I broke up with him on Christmas Eve. And because of the guilt I carry for doing that, I can't allow this holiday to be anything less than memorable for all the right reasons. Nobody needs to see me humiliate Ethel." I pointed my finger at them. "But that doesn't mean I won't if I decide I have no choice. My apartment is enormous, and it has a host of other rooms where I could school her in private. I'd be very discreet about it. No one would have to know."

"I think that's smart," Jennifer said. "You're back with Marcus. The memories you're creating with him now matter more than ever. There should be no public drama in sight."

"If you can pull it off, I agree," Lisa said. "And if you do need to dress her down, she might even say to hell with the party and leave."

"Which will only make things worse for you at home."

"No, it won't. I already told Tank if she tries anything at your party, his parents will have to pack their bags and find a hotel room because there is no way they'll be staying with us after that. He's so tired of his mother's behavior, he agreed."

"I'm just hoping the only reason Ethel said that was to get you worked up," Jennifer said. "Ethel loves her some mind games—and this could be one of them."

"And if it isn't, I'll deal with the situation discreetly," I said. "In the meantime, don't worry about it, Lisa. I want you and Tank to enjoy the party. If Ethel dares to try something, I'll handle it." I finished my glass of champagne. "But enough of that. I'm throwing a Christmas Eve party tomorrow night, and it's going to be epic. Earlier in the week, the three of us went to Bergdorf, where we bought beautiful shoes and gorgeous dresses, our men will look handsome in their new suits, everyone else knows they should dress to the nines, and Bernie has agreed to do our hair and makeup in the late afternoon."

"Is he still coming to the party?" Jennifer asked.

"He is."

"Then you should invite Addy," she said. "Now that he's tossed Tootie into the trash, you never know—they might hit it off."

"I love that idea," Lisa said.

"Let me talk with Bernie first," I said. "Years ago, he used to cut Addy's hair, so they know each other, which is good. But at some point—and without giving Bernie a reason—Addy started to see somebody else. I think it's because Bernie is openly gay. Sometimes he can also be a bit flamboyant. With Addy in the closet at the time, maybe he wasn't comfortable with that."

"But now that he's out of the closet, maybe Bernie is

exactly what he needs, even if they only become friends," Jennifer said. "You never know."

"I'll see what I can do."

"Is there anything we can help with while we're here?" Lisa asked.

"I don't think so," I said. "Thanks to Thomas, the apartment has been decorated. Housekeeping will be here in an hour to clean. And catering will be here tomorrow at six to set everything up. I think I'm good."

Later, when they left, I called Bernie, we talked about Addy, and to my surprise, it was *he* who suggested I invite him to the party—not me.

"Nobody wants to be alone at Christmas," he said. "Addy is a nice man. He's also quite handsome. I'm happy to hear he can finally get on with his life. I say you call and invite him."

When I did, I got my second surprise—Addy was all in.

TWENTY-FOUR
BARBARA

"You've outdone yourself," Marcus said as he took hold of my hand. We were strolling through the apartment for one final look before our guests arrived. "This is beyond impressive, Barbara—especially the attention to detail. You and Thomas smashed it. Well done."

I looked up at him and smiled. He was wearing a dark-gray Tom Ford houndstooth sport jacket; a light-gray cashmere turtleneck sweater; black dress pants by Dior Homme; and black boots by his favorite designer, Prada. If he thought the apartment looked beyond impressive, I thought *he* looked beyond handsome.

"Thank you," I said.

"And then there's your dress," he said as he admired me in it. "I've never seen you in something so dramatic."

"Do you like it?"

"I think it's sexy as hell."

I was wearing a full-length black maxi dress by Balenciaga. It fell to the floor, the sleeves were long, the fabric flowed beautifully when I moved, and the turtleneck was so long and elegant, I chose not to wear a necklace so that nothing could detract from it. The shoes, which you could barely see because the dress nearly covered them, were a pair of black Manolo Blahnik Lauren crystal-embellished mules with a pointed toe and a four-inch heel. In this dress, all you could see were the crystals on the toes, which I thought was perfect.

"What do you think of the music?" I asked.

"I like that you went classical," he said. "It's subtle. People will be able to have conversations and actually hear each other."

"It's *German Baroque Sacred Music for Christmas*," I said. "Bernie suggested it."

"And here I thought you were going to play 'Grandma Got Run Over by a Reindeer,'" he said.

"I'm not above it, Marcus—especially if we can change out 'Grandma' for 'Ethel.'"

"How are you going to handle her tonight?"

"I'm going to be polite."

"And if she isn't?"

"It all depends on what she says or does—if anything. There's always a chance she'll choose to behave."

"Here's hoping."

When we entered the kitchen, the two servers I'd hired were busy assembling hors d'oeuvres on my grandmother's shiny silver platters. They were handsome men in their early thirties, each beautifully dressed in black tuxedos.

"Looking good, gentlemen," I said.

"Thank you, Ms. Blackwell," they said at once.

"Let's start with the caviar and the *gougères*," I said.

"And I think also the pigs in a blanket since Aiden will be here, not to mention Daniella, Cutter, and Tank, whom I know adore them."

"Of course, Ms. Blackwell."

I checked my watch.

"Five minutes," I said to Marcus.

"Who will show first?"

"That's easy," I said. "Jennifer and Alex—they are never late. I left the guest list with the concierge and requested that he not call to alert me when each person arrives. If he did that, I'd be spending far too much time on the phone when I should be chatting with our guests. Instead, I asked him to just send everyone up when they got here."

"You've thought of everything," he said.

"I've tried," I said. "Now how about having a martini at the bar? I need to make sure the bartender is on point."

"Let's do it," he said.

As we walked toward the bar in the great room, it occurred to me that I'd been so busy with preparations for the party, I'd yet to ask Marcus how his day was. So I did.

"I might have done a little shopping," he said after he ordered two martinis for us from the bartender.

"You still had shopping to do?" I said.

"I did," he said. "But now my kids are done. Daniella and Alexa are done. Jennifer, Alex, Aiden, Lisa, and Tank are done." He took the two martinis the bartender offered him and handed one to me. We touched glasses and sipped. "And as of today, you also are done."

"This is excellent," I said to the bartender.

"Thank you, Ms. Blackwell."

I looked at Marcus.

"You cut it close."

He raised an eyebrow.

"Some things take time to get just right."

"Suddenly I'm intrigued."

"You should be," he said. "Not that I'm saying anything more on this subject."

"You're a horrible tease."

"I just know how your mind works. If I gave you more details, you would figure it out in a flash." From the entryway, one of the elevators dinged. "And I can't have that."

"Shall we see who's here?" I asked. "I think the party has begun."

"Are you ready for this?"

I took his hand and squeezed it.

"Actually, I'm more excited than I've been in a long time."

———

"NAN NAN!" Aiden exclaimed when he saw Marcus and me moving toward the foyer, where Jennifer, Alex, and Luciana were removing their coats and handing them to one of the waiters. "You look over the moon divoon!"

"Do I?" I asked as I bent down to kiss him on the forehead.

"You do!"

"Well, let me tell you this, Aiden—so do you."

He was wearing a suit that matched his father's—black jacket and pants, black shoes, white shirt, and a tie that was the same navy blue as his mother's dress.

"You nailed it," I said to Jennifer after I admired her dress. It was a sleeveless deep-blue Valentino crepe couture gown with crystal embellishments on the straps. The thigh-high side slit and the off-the-shoulder neckline were everything.

"You think?" she asked.

"Darling, I know—it's all about carrying that same shade of blue from your gown to their ties. Brilliant."

"Thank you," she said as Alex and Marcus shook hands. "And then there's your dress."

"What do you think?"

"I've never seen you look so beautiful."

"Well, thank you," I said.

"It's true," Alex said. "You look striking, Barbara."

"Doesn't she?" Marcus said.

"Now all of you are trying to make me blush," I said. "Something I haven't done in years."

"How many years?" Jennifer asked.

"Oh, I don't know, Jennifer—probably when a boy first kissed me when I was fourteen."

"Those are the details I need right now."

"Get another martini in me and I might tell you."

I walked over to greet Luciana, a petite woman whose youthful face and sparkling eyes defied her age. She might be fifty-two, but her brown skin was so beautiful, she looked more like thirty to me. And then there was the dress Jennifer had purchased for her to make sure she felt as if she fit in with the rest of the group tonight. It was a lovely long-sleeve sheath dress in red by Victoria Beckham.

"You look gorgeous, Luciana," I said.

"Thank you, Ms. Blackwell."

"It's Barbara," I said. "I'm so happy you could come."

"It's my pleasure to be here."

"Of course you're here," I said. "You're family. Now whenever you feel that Aiden might benefit from a nap, I have one of the bedrooms prepared for you. Just find me before he becomes too cranky, and I'll show you where it is."

"I will," she said.

The elevator dinged again, this time revealing Daniella and Cutter, who looked ridiculously in love. A moment later, it was Madison and Brock followed by Kate, Ben, and Alexa.

"Would you like me to start mixing with everyone in the great room?" Marcus asked as he placed his hand against the low of my back.

"We won't be much longer," I said. "And that crew can certainly find their way to the bar. I think we'll be fine here for a few more minutes." I looked at him. "Besides, I'd rather have you here with me."

He pulled me closer to him then, and in the comfortable silence that passed, I felt my love for him grow. Just feeling the warmth of his body against mine made me feel safe. Whole. Wanted.

It wasn't long before almost everyone was here, including Bernie and Addy, who looked especially dashing in their suits and who were in the midst of a hearty laugh when the elevator doors whisked open.

Seeing that alone made my heart happy. After we exchanged compliments and air kisses, they left for the great room just as Epifania and Rudman arrived.

"The Loose Cannon of the Park Avenue is the here, the cookie!" she said as they exited the elevator.

For a moment, we exchanged pleasantries and a few laughs before they moved into the great room. When ten minutes passed and there was no sign of Lisa, Tank, Harold, or Ethel, I decided they would need to see themselves in. I knew their tardiness had nothing to do with Tank or Lisa, who were always punctual, so I could only imaging it had to do with Ethel, who was likely holding them up intentionally, if only to get under my skin.

Before we left the foyer, I told Marcus my theory on why they were late.

"If that's true, she really is a piece of work," he said.

"Regardless, she's about to step foot into my apartment," I said. "At the very least, that should be somewhat intimidating, especially when she sees me, the views, and the decorations. Will she try to ruin my party when it's clear I'm at the top of my game?" I shrugged as we started toward the great room. "I guess we'll all have to wait and see . . ."

TWENTY-FIVE

BARBARA

When Marcus and I entered the room, I looked around for my daughters first.

While I did so, I saw Kate and Ben sitting at the Steinway piano with Ben's fingers hovering over the keyboard. Did he play? Later, I'd have to ask him if he did. At the bar, Brock and Madison were ordering drinks with Epifania and Rudman. Alex and Jennifer were standing at one of the floor-to-ceiling windows that over-looked the city and all of its twinkling lights.

To their right were Daniella and Cutter, who were admiring the room's main Christmas tree, which Marcus and I had decorated. Cutter had his arm around Daniel-la's waist in such a casual, loving way, I had to believe a marriage proposal would be coming at some point. And then there was Alexa, who was looking so sadly at the tree, you'd think I was the one who had given it its last rights, especially when she shook her head and turned to look at me with disappointment.

"How could you?" she said as Marcus and I

approached. "You said you wouldn't, Mom. You promised you'd buy one of those beautiful fake trees from Balsam Hill."

"I apologize," I said. "But you have to understand that this tree had already been cut down when I bought it, Alexa. Was I just to let it go to waste?"

"Change starts with the consumer," she said. "If nobody bought live Christmas trees and the demand shifted to fake trees, the industry would change, trees would be saved, and our climate would be better for it."

"I'll get one next year."

"Oh, you'll have one next year," she said. "Because I'll be the one buying it for you." She looked at Marcus. "I'm sorry you had to hear that, Marcus. It's just that saving the planet means everything to me."

"As it should," he said. "And by the way, Alexa, not to deflect from the conversation, but you look especially pretty tonight."

"She does," Daniella agreed. "And do you want to know why? It's because she reached out to ask for my help."

"And I'm glad I did," Alexa said. "I asked for something made from animal-derived recycled wool, and that's exactly what Daniella found for me."

"It's lovely," I said of Alexa's black jacket dress. It featured notch lapels, a single-breasted front, long sleeves, and an A-line silhouette. With her long dark hair pulled back into a high pony, I thought she looked terrific. After I gave equal time to moon over Daniella's V-neck crisscross-back gown by Alexander McQueen, which also was in black, I kissed each of them on the cheek.

"I'm extremely proud of you both," I said as a waiter came by with a tray filled with flutes of champagne. Marcus and I took one, as did the others. "There was a time when I couldn't leave you alone together without fearing one of you would wind up wounded or dead. But that's no longer the case. Seeing how you've grown not only as women but also as sisters who have come to respect each other makes your mother beyond happy—and maybe a little bit relieved."

When I lifted my glass to them, Marcus did the same.

"Cheers to each of you," I said. "And Merry Christmas."

"Well done, ladies," Marcus said.

"Thank you, Marcus," Daniella said. She looked at him for a moment before she cocked her head to one side. "Do you mind if I ask you a question?"

"Shoot," he said.

"You don't happen to have a supercute and super-single young man working for you, do you?"

"Are you trying to get rid of me?" Cutter asked.

"Not on your life," she said. "I'm trying to land a man for Alexa."

"Ah," he said. "Good to know."

"I mean, look at this place," Daniella said. "Love is clearly in the air. Why shouldn't Alexa have somebody special in her life?"

"Because the universe is conspiring against me?" Alexa said. "I've already said this to Mom, but how many tree huggers are you going to hunt down in Manhattan, Daniella? None, that's how many." She raised her glass. "That said, Wenn Environmental has an office in Washington State. Maybe I should just move there, get my flannel on, and find somebody woodsy."

"Maybe you don't have to," Marcus said. "There are plenty of interesting young men who work for me, Alexa. Let me ask around and see what I can do."

"I mean, I wouldn't be mad if you did," she said.

"Then I'll work on it, OK?"

Her face softened.

"You're the best."

"Marcus is totally the best," Daniella said. She turned to him. "Alexa and I are really happy you're back in our mother's life. We also missed you, you know?"

"I feel the same," he said. "But that's behind us now."

"Right? I mean, at this point, all you need to do is put a ring on it."

"Daniella," I warned, not wanting to put Marcus on the spot. But when I glanced over at him, he looked unfazed by her response, which wasn't the case for me.

"Well, it's true," she said.

"I could say the same for you and Cutter. Would you like me to go there?"

"Please do," Daniella said. "I mean, at this point in our relationship? We should be busy making babies."

"Babies?" Alexa said. "You want to bring a child into a world that's doomed to run out of food?"

"Alexa, it's Christmas," Daniella said. "Try not go all scorched Earth on us tonight, OK?"

"I'm just trying to raise awareness," she said. "Eight billion people, Daniella. Eight billion. That's the world's population. Before you know it, we'll have to eat one another just like they do in one of Lisa's books."

"Those people are zombies."

"And that should concern you," she said. "Why?" She leaned toward her sister. "Because they're eating our food."

And that's enough of that, I thought.

"Time to mingle," I said to Marcus. "Shall we visit with the other guests?"

"Absolutely," he said. "But this first."

He gave Daniella and Alexa a kiss on the cheek before he shook Cutter's hand.

"Have fun tonight," he said. "And Alexa?"

"What's that, Marcus?"

"Give me a few days and I'll be in touch."

"Find her a hot zombie," Daniella said.

"That would be impossible," I said as we began to step away. "After all, I hear they run cold . . ."

TWENTY-SIX

BARBARA

Nearly sixty minutes into the party, Marcus and I had chatted with everyone and were ordering our second martinis at the bar when I saw Lisa and Tank enter the great room, with Ethel and Harold in tow.

"Well, well," I said quietly to Marcus as a waiter began taking their coats. "Look who decided to show."

"Are you OK?"

"Never better."

"Are you sure?"

"I am."

Daniella, Cutter, and Alexa happened to be closest to them when they arrived, so I simply watched from afar as they greeted them.

"Lisa and Tank don't look too happy," Marcus said as he handed me my cocktail. "And neither does Harold."

"And then there's Ethel," I said to him. "Looking like she was just slapped by a stranger."

"Come again?"

"She looks stunned to be here."

"I see what you mean."

"I suppose we should go over and say hello."

"And I suggest we make quick work of it," Marcus said. "Get in, get out, get on with the party. The less time you spend with Ethel McCollister means the fewer chances she'll have to say something that might upset you. The party has been a lot of fun tonight. Don't let her destroy the mood and especially all your hard work. This is your first Christmas Eve in your new apartment. I want you to look back on this day with love and fondness, not with guilt or frustration. Sound like a plan?"

"That sounds perfect," I said.

When we walked over to greet everyone and Lisa and Tank looked at me first, I saw the tension in their eyes. I tried to calm whatever it was they were feeling by giving each of them a kiss on the cheek along with a warm greeting.

"I'm so glad you're here," I said to them.

"I'm sorry we're so late," Tank said. "I apologize, Barbara."

"As do I," Lisa said.

"But there are no apologies needed," I said. "I'm just happy you're here. Now the party can really begin."

After Marcus shook Tank's hand and gave Lisa a kiss on the cheek, I glanced at Harold and Ethel, who were looking around the great room with expressions that looked a lot like disbelief and awe.

"Harold? Ethel?" I said to them. "So happy you could drop by."

"We apologize for being late," Harold said as he shook my hand. "It wasn't our intention."

"It wasn't," Ethel offered in a chilly voice. "So sorry, Barbara."

The moment she said that, Marcus's words came to mind.

Get in, get out, get on with the party.

And he was right.

Wrap it up.

"You're here," I said. "That's all that matters. Welcome!" I motioned toward Marcus. "May I introduce you to the love of my life?"

"The love of your life?" Ethel said.

"That's right," I said, aware that Marcus was looking at me with new eyes. "Marcus Koch, please meet Ethel and Harold McCollister, Tank's parents."

"It's my pleasure," Marcus said.

As they shook hands, I quickly assessed Ethel's look. She was a tall reed of a woman somewhere in her early sixties, although to her credit, she appeared younger than she was. She had a coiffed helmet of blonde hair, her lips were painted deep red, and she was dressed completely in winter white—stylish wool slacks, a fitted blazer buttoned once at the waist, and a camisole that betrayed not one millimeter of cleavage.

If she was sitting on a cloud, she might be mistaken for an angel, which probably was her intent.

"Barbara," she said to me.

"Yes, Ethel?"

"Your apartment is nearly in the clouds."

"It sometimes feels that way," I said. "But we are on the ninetieth floor, so at least there's a reason for that."

"Did you choose this apartment for the sake of its

views?" she asked. "Or so you could be closer to our heavenly father?"

"Certainly not the latter," I said.

"Then perhaps *he* chose it for you."

"Anything's possible," I said lightly. "Especially if you're a believer, which I'm not. But that's a conversation for another day. Would anyone like a drink?"

"I'm a teetotaler," Ethel said.

"Even at church?" I said. "When they serve the wine?"

"It's not wine, Barbara. It's the blood of Christ."

"I see," I said. "Well, however you want to defend it. Harold?"

"I wouldn't mind a scotch," he said.

"I wish you wouldn't, Harold," Ethel said.

He turned to her. "After today? I'm having at least one, Ethel. Maybe even two."

"To be discussed when we return home," she said.

"Tank and I would love a cocktail," Lisa said.

"Of course you would, Lisa," Ethel said beneath her breath. "I'm surprised Barbara didn't gift you a pail of vodka when you stepped out of the elevator."

When Tank looked at her, Ethel may have avoided his eyes, but the tension between them only grew.

"Don't start," he said.

"I've started nothing, Mitchell," she said. "If I'm tense, it's only because I can't believe I'm here on the eve of Christ's birth when I already told all of you we should be attending mass."

"We're doing that at midnight," Harold said. "You know that."

"What I know, Harold, is that when we do go, you'll likely be drunk on that scotch you want so much."

"Leave it alone," Harold warned.

"And watch you become an alcoholic? I think not."

This is already going south, I thought. *I need to get Ethel alone. Lisa heard her say she wanted to destroy my party. For so many reasons, most of which come down to Marcus, I can't allow that to happen. He's acutely aware that three years ago today, I'm the one who ended our relationship. Tonight needs to be remembered not for that but as a celebration that we found our way back to each other. But Ethel alone could ruin that memory for us. In fact, if she really wanted to, she'd* become *the memory, which I can't allow.*

"Ethel," I said.

"Yes, Barbara?"

"Can I interest you in a tour of the apartment? There is a view from my office window I'd especially like you to see. It's beyond beautiful."

"Well, I'm not so sure," Ethel said after a moment. "Is your office loaded up with lilacs, Barbara? I understand that's a question nobody wants me to ask at such a festive event, but I've been fooled by you once before, and I promised myself that would never happen again."

"Mom," Tank said.

"It's true," she said. "I even took Benadryl before coming here tonight. Can anyone blame me? Trust is a fragile thing, and sometimes my PTSD gets the best of me."

"Then allow me to ease some of that for you," I said. "There are no lilacs in my apartment, Ethel. Nothing nefarious. My only wish for you and everyone else is to have a good time tonight." I motioned toward the hallway behind her. "Why don't we start doing that now?"

A silence passed before Ethel took a breath and appeared to resign herself to the situation.

"Lead the way," she said.

I gave Marcus a quick kiss on the lips, asked him if he'd take our guests to the bar, and started down the hallway with Ethel.

Straight into the unknown.

THERE WERE two ways I could play this—aggressively or calmly. While I wanted to go with the former, my gut told me to go with the latter.

And so I did.

At least for now.

"All of this is very pretty," she said as we walked toward my office, which was at the end of the hall. "With all of this glass, I can only imagine you don't suffer from a deficiency of vitamin D."

Somebody's milked one too many cows, I thought as we stepped into my office. *Or slaughtered one too many pigs.*

Whatever. Just go with it.

"When the sun is out, it can be quite bright in here," I said.

"I'm sure it can." She looked around the room as I clicked the door shut behind us. "So where is this view you wanted me to see, Barbara? Or is that even why we're here?"

"Actually, it isn't," I said. "You and I need to speak."

She narrowed her eyes.

"I was promised a pretty view."

I was about to clap back when she shrugged.

"But go ahead and say what you need to say to me."

I motioned toward the two facing sofas at the far left of the room. We sat on opposite couches, crossed our legs at the knee, and settled in for whatever was to come, which I already knew was a gamble. One wrong move could have us at each other's throats.

Be open with her about Marcus.

I was. And to her credit, Ethel listened to everything, especially why I needed this evening to go as smoothly as possible.

"So all of this is about love," she said.

"It is. When I ended my relationship with Marcus, it was on Christmas Eve. That was three years ago, and although neither of us will ever forget that night, Marcus is back in my life, and he deserves nothing but perfection tonight—from me, my family, and my friends."

"And what does that have to do with me?"

"I'll tell you. Earlier tonight, Marcus said he wanted me to look back on today with love and fondness, not frustration. I want the same for him."

"Again, what does this have to do with me, Barbara?"

"Ethel, let's not play games," I said. "You came here with an attitude. The moment I caught whiff of it, I brought you here before you could go any further than you already had."

"I have no idea what you are talking about."

"PTSD, Ethel?"

"Well, it's true," she said. "After all, you're the one who gave it to me."

This is going nowhere, I thought. *Shut her down now.*

"Let me be very straight with you," I said. "I need to know if I can count on you to make zero waves with anyone tonight. Because if you can't promise me that as a guest in *my* home? The moment you start doing so, I'll have no choice but to chalk this evening up as a loss and vilify you in front of everyone, which is something neither of us wants."

I met her stoic gaze with my own.

"If you even begin to cause trouble, I'll do it, Ethel. And in the end, I'll be throwing your ass out of my apartment with several choice words hurled at your back while everyone looks on."

"So you're threatening me, Barbara?"

"I'm trying to get through to you."

"While you do that, consider this—if you did that to me, Marcus would be looking on, likely wondering why he fought so hard to win back the love of a classless woman whose hatred knows no bounds. He'd start second-guessing everything."

"No, he wouldn't."

"Are you sure?"

"Marcus knows all about you."

"But how well does he know *you*?" she asked. "Because that's the real question, isn't it? Does he know what you did to me at my son's wedding? Does he know how vicious you were then and can be now? He likely has some idea, just not the full picture." She smiled sweetly. "Maybe I should fill him in."

"Don't come for my relationship, Ethel."

"I'm ruling out nothing."

A flash of rage swept through me when she said that, but I refused to show it. Instead, I leaned back on the sofa as calmly as I could and collected my thoughts before I went in for the kill.

"You have a tenuous relationship with your son, don't you?" I asked.

"Once again, I have no idea what you're talking about, Barbara."

"Yes, you do. You know Tank only tolerates you. You know how much he loathes it when you insult his wife with your Bible bullshit. How long do you think he'll allow you to remain in his life if you continue to show him just how vicious *you* are? Relationships end, Ethel, and from everything I've heard, you've pushed yours with your son to the limit."

"Heard from who?"

"Who do you think?" I said. "Tank and Lisa aren't just my friends; they're also an important part of my life. We talk daily, for God's sake. Do you do the same? There's no need to answer, because I already know you don't. Tank especially tries to evade you because he's sick of how you undermine Lisa. He also knows there's nothing that would make you happier than to see his marriage dissolve."

She moved to speak, but I stopped her by charging forward.

"If you try to defame me in front of Marcus, your son

will bear witness to all of it. And what in the hell do you believe he's going to think of you then? That one day you might try to undermine him and Lisa? I promise that's exactly what he'll be thinking. Hell, even fearing."

I shook my head.

"For a woman who claims to live her life with God in her heart, if you come for Marcus and me tonight, your behavior will only reveal just how dark and rotted that heart is. Whether you want to expose that to your son is on you, Ethel. So choose. I'm beyond ready to go head-to-head with you."

She went silent as she absorbed everything I just said to her. I was worried she was going to go off on me, but to my surprise, she didn't. Instead, she let out a long, low, exasperated sigh.

"Clearly, neither of us is going to win this battle," she said. "And so be it. If I'll be dealing with you for the rest of my life, which it appears I will be, the exhaustion of rehashing this time and again isn't worth it. At least for me it isn't. But I will say this, Barbara—I'm walking away from this knowing I have the Lord on my side, which never will be the case for you."

"And trust me when I say this, Ethel—having Marcus at my side trumps all that." And that was it. As far as I was concerned, this conversation was over. "I know we'll never move beyond this," I said as I stood. "But we certainly can behave as if we have."

She also stood.

"You're the better liar," she said. "But I'll try my best."

She moved toward the door but then stopped and turned to me.

"Harold and I will be leaving shortly," she said. "As an excuse, I'll tell everyone the truth—I've become sick to my stomach. But in the meantime, don't worry, Barbara. I'll be on my best behavior."

"As will I," I said as I followed her out of my office so that I could rejoin my guests.

But can I trust her? I wondered as we walked down the hallway toward the great room, where I could hear the din of people talking and laughing. *And what will I do if it turns out that I can't?*

TWENTY-SEVEN
BARBARA

It didn't take long for me to realize I could trust Ethel—at least this time—because fifteen minutes after our talk, she and Harold announced they were leaving.

"My apologies," she said to my guests and me. "I don't know why, but suddenly I've become sick to my stomach. I should probably leave." She placed her hand over her abdomen. "The nausea is only getting worse."

Marcus was standing next to me and reached for my hand.

"Tank?" Harold said.

"What's that, Dad?"

"Your mother and I will take a cab back to your place. Could I have the key?"

"Of course." Tank reached into his right pocket, removed the key, and handed it to his father. "You remember the code to the alarm?"

"I do."

"I'm sorry to see you go, Dad."

"So am I, son. But maybe this will pass and we can enjoy the rest of the evening when you and Lisa return home. If not, there's always tomorrow."

When they left, I was aware of the shift in the mood —nobody was mixing or talking—so I was beyond grateful when Aiden came out of nowhere and ran past everyone with poor Luciana hot on his heels.

"Aiden," she said. "Please stop running. You might break something. This isn't your home."

"But it's Christmas!" he said as he darted left into the kitchen. "And nobody can catch me but Santa or his elves!"

"Then consider me one of his elves," she called out.

"But you're not, so just try to catch me! Just try! Ahahahahahaha!"

"Holy to the moly," Epifania said. "That keed got the turbocharge!"

"You don't even know," Jennifer said to her. "Because what you just saw? That's nothing."

"She's not joking," Alex said. "There are times when I think he could take flight."

"Is everything OK?" Marcus asked me in a low voice.

"It is now," I said.

"You're happy she's gone?"

"I'm thrilled she's gone."

"Can we have a moment alone?"

I looked up at him, saw how serious he was, and nodded.

"Would my bedroom work?" I asked.

"It would."

Is he angry with me? I wondered as we left the great room and started down the hallway. *Does he think I took things too far with Ethel?*

I wasn't sure, but when we stepped into my bedroom, I felt unusually on edge when Marcus closed the door, locked it, and then faced me as I flipped a switch to turn on the lights.

"I can't do this anymore," he said.

When he said those words, I felt the bottom of my stomach fall away.

"You can't do what anymore?" I said. "*Us?*"

"No, not us," he said. "Never not us."

"Then what?"

"Before you left to speak with Ethel, you said I'm the love of your life."

"You are."

"But then you just walked away."

"I had no choice," I said. "She was already starting to stir the pot. I needed to shut her down before she took things too far."

"I understand that," he said. "But, Barbara, when you publicly share something as monumental as that with everyone in the room—something you haven't even said personally to me—you have to know all I wanted to do at that moment is this."

When he leaned down to kiss me, I could feel nothing but his love for me pouring out of his heart and soaring straight into mine.

"Because I feel the same way," he said in my ear. "You're the love of *my* life. These past three years have been hell without you in it."

"I'm so sorry," I said.

"Don't be," he said. "You had every right to do what you did. I get it. I fixed it. I'm just happy we're finally beyond it. I'm relieved we're now where we're supposed to be."

"I feel the same."

"I wish I could take you now," he said as he wrapped his arms around my waist. "How long before everyone leaves?"

"Do you want me to send them away, too?" I asked.

"Would you?"

I smiled.

"I mean, it would be rude of me if I did, but I certainly could."

"No," he said. "You're right. And besides, keeping me waiting longer is only going to make me more insatiable later."

"If you keep talking to me like that, I'm going to have to change my panties, Marcus."

"Let me change them for you," he said as he pressed his erection hard against my thigh. "With my teeth."

"If we don't join everyone now, it's never going to happen," I said. "Shall we?"

He kissed me before taking a step back.

"Give me a moment," he said. "You reapply your lipstick in the bathroom, I'll think about Ethel in her birthday suit, and before you know it?" He motioned toward his bulging crotch. "This won't be an issue."

"That's never been an issue for me."

"Talking about it is not going to soften the situation."

"Right," I said. "I'll rejoin you in a moment."

After I touched up my makeup in the bathroom, I returned to the bedroom. Marcus reached for my hand, and together we left the room feeling more in love than ever.

TWENTY-EIGHT
BARBARA

As we started down the hall, I saw Lisa and Tank talking at the far end of the corridor. Before they turned to us, I could sense their frustration and embarrassment, anger and disappointment.

And all due to one woman who refused to leave well enough alone.

"Barbara, we're sorry," Tank said as we approached them. "We never should have brought my mother here. That was a mistake."

"There's no need for an apology, Tank," I said. "Because let's be honest—what were you supposed to do? Leave her at home on Christmas Eve? And then face her wrath when you returned?" I shook my head. "You did the right thing. And before either of you ask what was said between your mother and me in private, why don't we just move on and enjoy the rest of the evening? I know I'd like that."

"Then that's what we'll do," Lisa said. "Thank you, Barbara."

"No worries," I said. "In fact, it's just that sort of blip I had with Ethel that martinis were designed to fix." I looked up at Marcus. "Join me at the bar?"

"Absolutely," he said.

I looked at Lisa and Tank's hands, which were empty.

"Please have one with us," I said.

"An excellent idea," Tank said. "Lead the way."

When we moved into the great room, I was happy to see that everyone appeared to be enjoying themselves. The waiters were circling the room with fresh hors d'oeuvres, Brock and Madison were chatting with Alexa, Daniella, and Cutter at one end of the sofa, and Jennifer and Alex were at the Christmas tree laughing with Bernie and Addy.

"Look at Addy," I said. "I've never seen him so relaxed."

"That's the power of finally being able to live your truth," Lisa said. "It's also the power of Bernie. He's probably telling one of his racy little stories, which means I'm officially jealous I'm not there to hear it."

"Why don't you both go over and say hello?" Marcus said. "Tank and I will get the drinks."

"We'll be right back with your martinis."

"They're the best," Lisa said as we watched them walk toward the bar.

When Marcus placed his hand on Tank's shoulder, I knew it was out of a clear show of support. "I couldn't agree more," I said. "We are very lucky, my dear. Not everyone has a Tank and a Marcus in their lives."

"I couldn't imagine mine without Tank in it," she

said. "It would be so empty." She looked at me. "Is that how you're beginning to feel about Marcus?"

"It is," I said.

"Really?"

"Mm-hmm."

"I'm so happy for you, Barbara."

"I know you are," I said. "And I appreciate it, Lisa. Because I never thought I'd be this lucky."

"It was meant to be." She looked over at Bernie, Addy, Jennifer, and Alex. "Let's go over and see what Bernie is up to," she said. "Because now he has Addy laughing. Jennifer will tell me what he said later, but it won't be the same. She doesn't have Bernie's . . . flair."

"Darling, a bejeweled butterfly doesn't have Bernie's flair," I said as we approached them.

And then Bernie paused to look at me.

"Did you just compare me to a bejeweled butterfly, Barbara?" he asked.

"You don't miss a thing, do you, darling?"

"Not when I hear my name thrown into the mix, I don't."

"You heard correctly," I said.

"I see," he said. "Well then. Hmm. How curious. A bejeweled butterfly over a festooned queen, Addy? I suppose if I had an ounce of moisture left in my body, I'd shed a tear." He looked at me. "Good thing I don't."

"What were you saying to make Addy laugh?" Lisa asked. "Tell me it was one of your stories, because you know I live for them."

"You only live for the questionable ones," he said.

"True enough."

"Which officially makes you a hag."

"A hag?"

"A fag hag, darling, but in the best, most positive use of the phrase." He looked around the room. "You're hardly alone. I mean, Barbara is the queen of all fag hags, but there are a couple of princesses in the mix. Jennifer is one. Daniella and Epifania are absolutely as well. I don't know Kate or Madison well enough to be sure, but they certainly have promise. And then there's you, Lisa." He winked at her. "Shine on, sweetie."

"Just hearing that makes me feel as if I've finally made something of my life," she said.

"You know?" I said. "I think that's the saddest thing I've ever heard. Brava for aiming so low, Lisa—well done!"

"Take your martini," Lisa said as Marcus stepped beside me with two shimmering glasses in his hands. "And since you're so sad, I suggest you drown your sorrows in that."

After I took my drink from Marcus and touched glasses with him, I glanced at Addy, who was clearly trying to suppress a smile.

"How are you, Addy?" I asked.

"Never better, Barbara."

"Is this too much bitchiness for you?"

"Not at all," he said. "In fact, I have to say, I've waited decades to be part of something so fun."

My heart went out to him then, and as much as I wanted to know how things were going between him and Tootie, I didn't press. When he was ready to discuss his pending divorce, he would. In the meantime, I just wanted to make sure he was enjoying himself and that he knew he was in a safe space with us.

Trust will come later.

"I don't want to go, but we should probably leave," Jennifer said to Alex. "It's past eleven. If Santa is going to pay a visit, we need to get Aiden down soon." She looked over at me. "I hope that's OK with you, Barbara."

"It's fine," I said. "I remember those days all too well. Let me call everyone over so that they can say something nice to you before you leave."

"That's one way to put it," Alex said.

"There are other ways, Alex," I said. "But since it's Christmas, I'll refrain."

"You're killing me," Marcus said after I motioned for everyone to gather around the tree.

"Softly?" I asked.

"If you want me to call you Roberta, I'm happy to do so."

"Barbara will do," I said.

"Just Barbara?"

"Well, what else is there?" I said—and then I narrowed my eyes. "Don't you dare say Rita."

"Actually, I was thinking of something more meaningful."

"Meaningful?"

"That's right," he said with a smile. "Like Barbara Koch."

And just like that, he dropped to one knee in front of me.

There were several audible gasps.

My heart began to quicken.

In shock, I looked over at Jennifer and Alex, Daniella and Alexa, Lisa and Tank. Each had tears in their eyes.

"Barbara?" Marcus said.

When I looked down at him, I saw the raw emotion in his eyes before I noticed the enormous pear-shaped diamond engagement ring he was holding out to me in a black velvet box.

"Marry me," he said.

Those were two words I never thought I'd hear again, and yet there they were.

"I want to spend the rest of my life with you," he said. "I want to marry you, I want you to be my wife, and I want to make it official."

After I divorced Charles, I told myself I'd never marry again. But that was years ago. And back then? I never thought I'd meet anyone like Marcus.

Follow your heart.

And so I did.

"Yes," I said to him. "Of course I'll marry you, Marcus."

"*Heyzeus Cristo!*" Epifania said. "It's a Christmas miracle!"

As my daughters and friends started to cheer and clap, Marcus stood, put the ring on my finger, and then sealed the deal with the most searing kiss we'd ever shared.

"Mission accomplished," he said in my ear.

"Is that what you were on?" I asked.

"Oh, I was on a mission, Barbara. There was no way I was going to screw this up again."

I ran my fingers through his hair.

"Thank you," I said.

"For what?"

I kissed him on the lips.

"For coming back for me. And for putting up with me until I could no longer deny my love for you."

"I love you," he said.

"I love you more."

I was aware of waiters coming over with bubbling flutes of champagne on round silver trays.

"Everyone, please take one," Alex said as Jennifer handed him a glass. "I'd like to make a toast." When each guest had a glass, he raised his to Marcus and me. "Being married to Jennifer has taught me that love is just a word until someone comes along to give it meaning," he said. "That's what you two have found, and I'm beyond happy for you. Congratulations, Barbara and Marcus. Anyone can catch your eye, but it takes someone special to catch your heart. I know that to be true. And looking at you now? It's clear that you do as well." He lifted his glass even higher. "Can we all say cheers to that?"

"Cheers!" everyone said.

"Now I'm going to cry," I said as I sipped my champagne. "Something I never do."

"Can I offer a toast as well?" Daniella said.

"Of course you can," I said, already knowing that this one might push me over the edge. Before she spoke, she reached for Cutter's free hand and squeezed it.

"I always knew you'd find love again," she said to me. "What I never imagined is that when you did, he'd be as wonderful as Marcus." She looked at him. "Marcus, when I say this, I know I also speak for Alexa," she said.

"Thank you for making our mother feel secure enough to give love another chance. Because after divorcing our father, that's exactly what she needed, and we're thrilled she found it in you."

"Thank you, Daniella," he said.

"No, thank you," she said with a smile. "And welcome to our family." She looked over her shoulder at Alexa. "Would you like to say something?"

"I would," Alexa said.

She focused her attention on me.

"You deserve this," she said. "All of it. I know you never thought you'd find love again—let alone get married again—but today we know better. You found your soul mate, Mom. Hell, you found a man even Daniella and I can agree upon, so consider that." When everyone laughed, Alexa simply shrugged before she turned to Marcus. "It was easy for my sister and me to embrace you," she said. "Not only can we see how much you love our mother but also we can feel her love for you." She lifted her glass of champagne to us. "You don't know it, but you've inspired me to believe that one day, I might be as fortunate as you. Congratulations!" she said. "I love you both."

I placed my hand over my heart. "You two have no idea how much your support has meant to me."

"We love you, Mom," Daniella said.

Alexa blew me a kiss.

"More than you know," she said.

"And I love all of you," I said as I looked around the room. "I'm beyond grateful you were part of an evening I never saw coming but will remember forever."

"Forever is a long time," Marcus said.

When I turned to him, I felt the rush of a brand-new start. "And yet it's nevertheless how long I plan to be married to you."

When he leaned down to kiss me, it occurred to me that if you want to spend the rest of your life with somebody, the rest of your life should start as soon as possible. What was the point of waiting? Because of me, we'd already lost three years. Our wedding would come, but our living situation could change as soon as possible.

Eight days later, it did.

EPILOGUE

On New Year's Day, which I thought was the perfect time to mark the beginning of our new lives together, my apartment officially became *our* apartment after Marcus finished moving into it.

It had been quite a week.

A thrilling week.

One of the happiest weeks of my life.

The day after Christmas, we hired a moving company and had worked tirelessly alongside them until the last box was unpacked.

That had been yesterday morning.

Now, after working together yesterday afternoon and deep into New Year's Eve, the largest spare bedroom had been turned into his office.

The library had been filled with his favorite books.

His clothes and shoes had been placed in his primary closet.

And next week? His old apartment would be put on the market for someone else to purchase and enjoy.

"We did it," Marcus said.

It was morning, and we were still in bed. Even though I'd slept, I'd be lying if I said I felt rested. In fact, every muscle in my body seemed as if it was on fire.

"I can't stop staring at the ceiling," I said.

"What's on the ceiling?"

"That's the thing," I said. "There's nothing on it. I'm just too tired to move my eyes."

"I get it," he said. "My hair hurts."

"Can hair even hurt?"

"Why not?" he said. "Everything else does."

"I'd reach for my hair to see if it also hurts, but I can't lift my arms."

"Imagine me giving you a massage."

"Imagine me shaving your head."

"Don't make me laugh."

"It's what I do."

"I know it is, but just not now, OK?"

"Fine," I said. "Your loss. I need to use the bathroom."

"Just remember the bathroom isn't the bed."

"I'm a goddamned lady."

"No," he said. "What you are is one hell of a woman."

"You think so?"

"I know so."

"Good. I'm also going to be one hell of a wife."

"And I'm going to be one hell of a husband."

"*My* husband."

"*My* wife."

"I love the sound of that."

"I love it more."

"You're so competitive."

"A trait I share with you."

"So you do."

"Should we call the concierge and ask for help?"

"First of all, I can't move. Second, I'm not telepathic."

"We're screwed."

"For the past week, we've behaved as if we're twenty."

"I thought we were smart."

"We are smart," I said. "We were just overly motivated."

"It was worth it."

"I'd smile at that, but I can't."

"Have you wet the bed yet?"

"Ask me that again and you'll have your answer."

"I'm going to attempt to get up."

"Good luck with that."

The bed stirred—and then it stopped.

"I tried and I failed."

"Sorry about that."

"What's next for us?"

"Rigor mortis?"

"I'm being serious."

"All right," I said. "Don't you know?"

"I mean, I can guess. Our wedding?"

"That's right," I said. "Our wedding."

"It's going to be epic."

"It's going to be all of that."

"People will cry."

"Doves will fly."

"Ethel will—"

"Don't say it," I said. "She won't be there."

With surprising ease, he turned onto his side and kissed me full on the mouth. "I can't wait to marry you, Barbara."

"I can't wait either," I said with a full heart. "But unlike you, I'm not joking. I honestly can't move, Marcus. Carry me to the bathroom?"

"Now the romance really begins," he said with a laugh.

"Don't mock me."

"I love you too much to mock you," he said as he stood and walked over to my side of the bed. "But just so you know, this might hurt."

"The fact that you're naked is all the distraction I need."

"Happy to help," he said. "Ready?"

"To spend the rest of my life with you? That would be a hard yes. To get off this bed? Not so much." When I looked into his eyes, I saw the man I never should have doubted. The man I would one day be lucky enough to call my husband. "Be gentle with me?" I asked.

Before he answered, his expression turned serious.

"Always," he said as he lifted me off the bed. "And forever, Barbara. You can count on it."

When I rested my head against his shoulder, I was overcome with gratitude, because there was no question in my mind that I could count on that from him—and so much more.

UNTITLED

Thank you for reading *A Very Blackwell Christmas*! I hope you enjoyed Barbara's second-chance romance. Look for a new book to be released in 2023.

If you would leave a review of this or any of my books, I'd appreciate it. Reviews are critical to every writer. Please leave even the shortest of reviews. And thank you for doing so!

XO,
    Christina

Printed in Great Britain
by Amazon